SHADOWED
by
PROPHECY

A CROWN OF THE PHOENIX PREQUEL NOVELLA

BOOK ONE

C.A. VARIAN

Editing: Willow Oak Author Services

Cover: JV Arts

Formatting: Me!

Page Edge Design by Painted Wings Publishing

CONTENTS

EKOTORIA

Aegricia
Marella Arch
Norithae
Spectre Forest
Elder Sea
Undying Desert
Diapolis
Warbotach

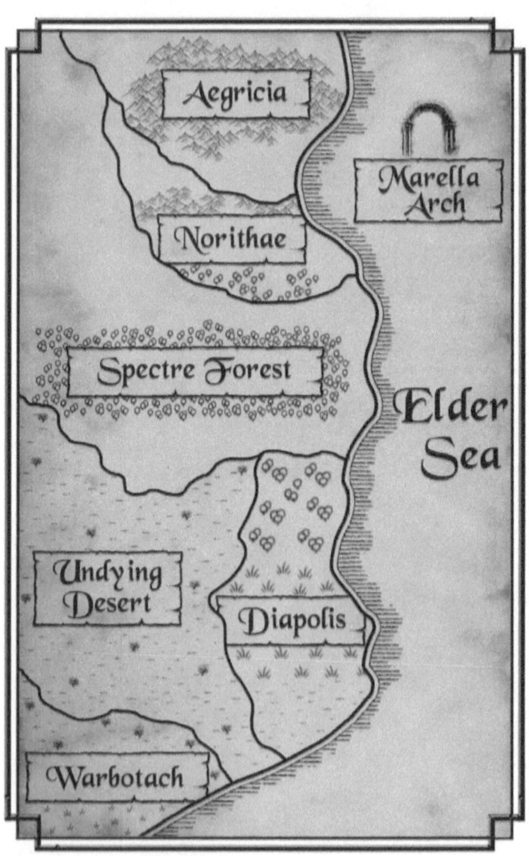

INAS

Breqan
El-Wahba
Monen
Kotol
Illever
Harmuz
Sea
Howling Forest
Marella
Arch
Vaekros

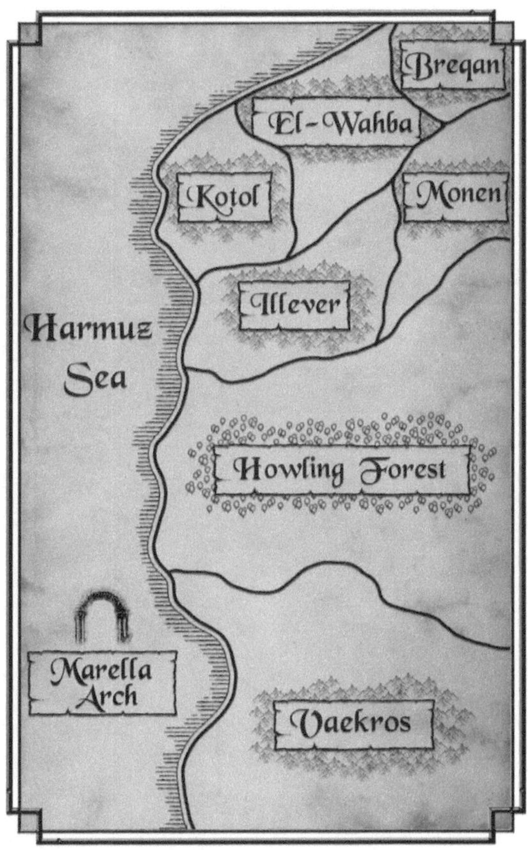

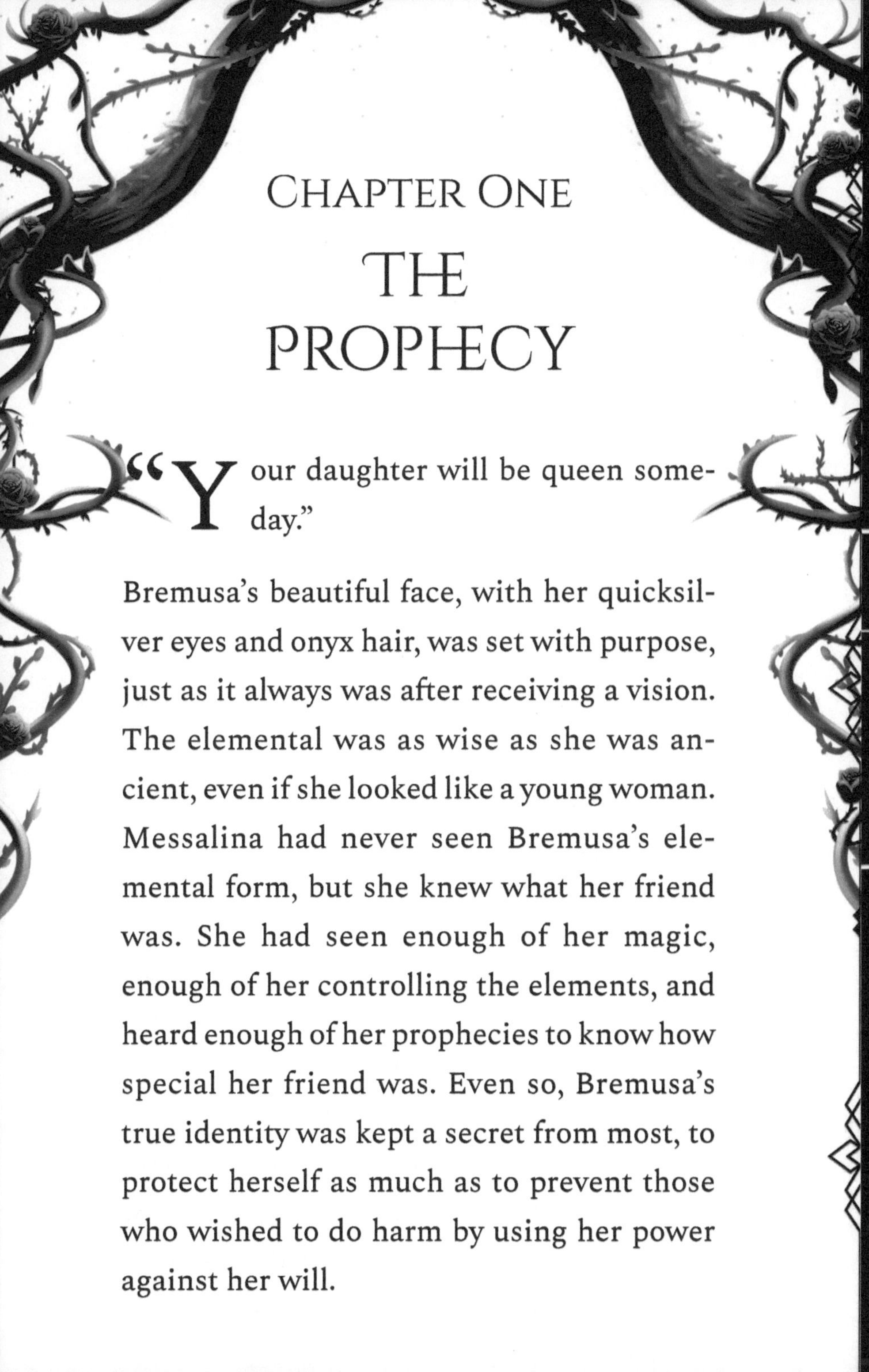

CHAPTER ONE
THE PROPHECY

"Your daughter will be queen some-day."

Bremusa's beautiful face, with her quicksilver eyes and onyx hair, was set with purpose, just as it always was after receiving a vision. The elemental was as wise as she was ancient, even if she looked like a young woman. Messalina had never seen Bremusa's elemental form, but she knew what her friend was. She had seen enough of her magic, enough of her controlling the elements, and heard enough of her prophecies to know how special her friend was. Even so, Bremusa's true identity was kept a secret from most, to protect herself as much as to prevent those who wished to do harm by using her power against her will.

Messalina Lumino clasped her cape at her throat. "Otera would be a better queen than me. The crown will choose her." The words rang true as Messalina said them. Her older sister, Otera, would've been the more obvious choice for queen. She was smarter and she was braver. She had a sharp tongue that would send any man to his knee.

Bremusa shot her a sidelong glance as she lifted her hood over her head. "The crown chooses, and, as I have said before, it has already chosen you. Otera would make an excellent queen, but the crown's favor cannot be forced. It will choose you, and your daughter after."

Knowing her friend was always right, Messalina dropped the conversation. Instead of the throne being passed down through bloodlines, as was commonplace in the rest of their world, the Aegrician crown chose the queen. The Kingdom of Aegricia, led by queens instead of kings, controlled the portal between the magical fae realm and the

human realm, and was the most powerful crown in their world, probably in any world.

The Aegrician military were the gatekeepers, and the crown always chose who would best protect the passage through the portal. Passage into the human realm could only be made by their people, by the women who could shift into their phoenix forms and fly through the portal. Even though the portal allowed passage into the human lands, they were no longer permitted to do so by the human kings and queens. A treaty set long ago in a joint council between the fae realm and the human realm put those rules into place. To prevent war between the realms, which had seemed imminent even then, control of the portal had been placed in the hands of the Aegricians due to their proximity to the Marella Arch, the portal itself, and the stability of its monarchy.

Even so, if the crown chose her, Messalina knew she would serve her kingdom proudly and would surround herself with those who could guide her in how best to protect the sanctity of the portal. But until that time came, she could still hope it would choose someone else.

The cobblestone street crunched below Messalina and Bremusa's boots as they left the palace's courtyard and headed toward the market. The air was chilly. Although the climate was typically colder in their place in the north of the continent of Ekotoria, it was clear that winter was coming. Messalina wrapped her arms around her body beneath her cloak. The long-sleeved wool tunic she wore wasn't quite warm enough to keep out the chill.

As she usually did, her older sister Otera had remained in court with their mother and grandmother as Messalina and Bremusa left the palace. Messalina hated the pageantry of court, even if the matriarch of her family, and their current queen, always insisted she show up. There was always some party, some male they wanted to match her with, but none of it interested her. If Messalina could have chosen her fate, she would have begged for feathered wings to burn from her back, and for a sword held firmly in her hand. The phoenix warriors of Aegricia were the fiercest in the land, and every part of her wished it had been her destiny, but her back remained ordinary, and her hands too dainty, so the choice wasn't hers.

Although all who resided in Aegricia were fae, just as were all the inhabitants of their continent, not all Aegricians were born with the ability to shift into phoenixes. Only women were given that honor, the ability to transform and soar into the sky, and only those women who were destined to be warriors. Messalina and her sister, Otera, were not born to be warriors, although both sisters wished they had been. The closest thing the sisters had to crimson feathers was their crimson hair, which they wore with pride.

"Is Otera interested in any of the males your mother has set her up with?" Bremusa's tone was playful. She already knew the answer to that question.

"You know Otera isn't interested in any of them. Maybe she'll choose to remain single forever." Bremusa and Otera were similar in that regard.

Bremusa snorted. "You're probably right. I could see her as an old spinster. I'll be a spinster right there with her. We can live in a hut together filled with woodland creatures."

Messalina snickered as they turned the corner and the market street came into view. Maybe her sister and best friend intended to grow old and stay single, but she wanted it all. She wanted a husband and children one day, more than she ever wanted to be queen. Unfortunately, if the crown chose her, those dreams may only ever be just that. Dreams.

The Kingdom of Aegricia's capital city of Flamecliff was built in the Aegrician mountains, but it was also a prospering port city supported by jewel crafting, textiles, farming, and mining. Out of all the kingdoms on their continent of Ekotoria, Messalina was glad to have been born in Aegricia. It may not have beaches as beautiful as the capital city of Diapolis, the mer kingdom on the southernmost coast, but the snow-capped mountains were ethereal, and the Spectre Forest held more magic than anywhere on the continent. The neighboring kingdom of Norithae was lovely and had the most handsome men on the continent with their big, leathery wings and tan skin, but nowhere else on the continent had the Aegrician peaks. She gazed at monuments as they walked, the scene picturesque as it framed the palace, she called home. Messalina checked the hood on her cloak as they approached the row of shops, stopping outside the tavern.

From the outside, the Singing Lantern Tavern looked inviting and folksy. Stones and giant tree trunks made up most of the building's outer structure, both resources taken from the mountains and the surrounding Spectre Forest, which spanned a large portion of the continent. They couldn't see through the stained-glass windows, but they

already knew the tavern would be busy. It always was.

As the two women entered the tavern through the heavily worn wooden door, they were welcomed by cheerful singing and the smile of the barmaid. Although Otera never joined them in the tavern, Messalina and Bremusa loved visiting the lively spot. Just as expected, the tavern was packed. Most of the patrons appeared to be traders or merchants who were either visiting the kingdom on foot or through the port that took in ships from the Elder Sea. Even with all of those who were not locals, Messalina nodded at a table of tavern regulars who recognized her even with her heavy hood throwing her face into shadows.

Choosing to maintain their anonymity to most of the patrons, they took a seat at their preferred table in the back corner of the tavern. Messalina scanned the crowd while waiting for the barmaid to bring their usual Aegrician whiskey, making sure there were no patrons in the building who could

cause trouble for them. Even with her grandmother being the current queen, there were still those who wished her harm, or at least wished to make her life more difficult. If it were up to her grandmother and the palace guards, she wouldn't be allowed to visit the tavern at all. A life secluded behind the palace walls was one she could never fathom, even if being the queen's granddaughter made her a target to those who wanted to cause trouble for the kingdom. Presently there was peace on their continent, but it hadn't always been that way, and there was no guarantee that peace would remain.

The barmaid, a short and stout middle-aged woman with tight black curls, dropped two mugs of whiskey on their table before scurrying away to wait on another table. Messalina took a sip of her drink, the whiskey like liquid fire pouring down her throat. A male in the corner of the tavern played a lute, singing a tune about a lost love as a group entered the tavern and sat at the bar. She watched them out of the corner of her eye as

Bremusa chatted about the upcoming winter solstice and what new guard had her eye. Messalina couldn't seem to pay attention to her friend as a familiar figure with chestnut hair and golden eyes caught her attention, making her blood run cold. *Joneira.*

CHAPTER TWO
DREAMS OF ADVENTURE

The only daughter of the Eternus noble family, Joneira had been raised to rule. With the Aegrician crown being placed upon the heads of those chosen by the crown itself, there was no expectation for it to be passed down through family lines. The Eternus family had never sat on the Aegrician throne, but it was well known how badly they wanted to.

Joneira's father, a successful merchant specializing in the trade of jewels mined from the Aegrician mountains, and her mother, a noble in her own right, ran in many prestigious social circles in the kingdom. Her family had wealth and power.

The one thing Messalina didn't know was how far Joneira's family would go to ensure the crown went to their daughter when the current queen died, or when the crown chose another.

Since their people could live for centuries, the crown often chose the next queen before the present one passed away, ensuring that power did not become corrupt by staying in the hands of one person for centuries, and allowing the current queen her much-deserved years of rest. Messalina's grandmother, Elowen Lumino, had been the Aegrician queen for ninety-nine years, so the crown would choose again within the year.

It was no secret that Messalina's grandmother wanted the crown to pass down to one of her granddaughters, just as Joneira's family wanted it to pass down to her, but neither family could control the outcome. The crown chose who the next queen would be. That was nonnegotiable. What Joneira's family didn't know, however, was that the Elemental's prophecy spoke of Messalina and her daughter, the latter of which would unify the northern kingdoms of the continent under one crown, to protect the portal from all who wished to exploit it. The Eternus family didn't know Bremusa's true identity, and they needed to keep it that way.

Checking to make sure that her hood was secure around her face, Messalina turned back to her friend and whispered across the table. "We need to get out of here before Joneira sees us. I don't want any trouble with her today."

Bremusa nodded, although it was obvious the female was not happy about having to leave when they'd only just gotten there. Rising from the table, the two friends turned down the hall and exited out the back door and into the alleyway that would lead them to the palace.

When they'd gotten far enough down the street to no longer have to worry about being seen by the controversial female, Messalina pulled her hood off to let the sunlight kiss

her face. Winter would be upon them soon, and with the winter came the snow. There were not many more sunny days ahead of them to look forward to.

"What do you want to do now?" Bremusa hesitated for a moment. "You know you're going to have to confront her eventually, Lina."

Messalina knew her friend was right, but she didn't trust herself to confront Joneira. She wasn't like her sister, wasn't bold enough to start conflicts, or even finish them. It was one more reason why she didn't feel she was the best person to become queen. Shrugging, she turned down the side road that led to the harbor, instead of the palace, with her friend following closely behind.

"A bunch of new ships came into the harbor today. We can go see what goods they've brought in. I could use a new sword belt and Sugarflash needs a new brush."

Bremusa snickered as she shook her head. "You spoil that horse, and I know exactly

why you want to go down to the harbor. It has nothing to do with buying accessories."

Messalina's jaw dropped in mock offense, a gasp leaving her mouth. "I have no idea what you mean."

She knew exactly what Bremusa was alluding to, but it was easier to pretend not to. Her dark-haired friend shot her a sideways glance. "You want to go down there and look at all the handsome merchants and pirates, hoping one of them will sweep you off this continent and away from its crown, its courts, suitors, fancy balls, and the competitive noble families who want to take your grandmother's throne and her head with it. Shall I go on?"

Making sure her aim was perfect, Messalina smacked her friend on her back, just enough to make her nearly trip, but not enough to make her fall over. "No. You should not go on, and you're wrong. I *would not* leave with a pirate. *Well*—maybe if he takes care of his teeth. And takes regular baths. *Otherwise* I would not leave with a pirate."

Bremusa laughed but she meant every word. Going on a high seas adventure sounded a much better use of her time than dressing in finery and being judged if she stepped a pedicured toe out of line.

They'd just nearly made it to the docks when a whistle caught their attention. Messalina's heart clenched along with her jaw, but she turned around anyway, Bremusa doing the same, their cloaks fluttering around their ankles in the breeze.

"I expected you to run straight back into your grandmother's silken skirts when you saw me, Messalina. Her time is almost up, after all." The smirk on Joneira's face sent Messalina seething deep in her belly but she tried to hide it from her face. The four males flanking the aspiring queen all seemed incredibly amused by her verbal jab.

Messalina, however, was not amused and opened her mouth to speak, but closed it again as Bremusa grabbed her arm. "Come on, Lina. We have places to be. She isn't worth your time."

She allowed her friend to lead her away, but not before shooting Joneira a toothy grin. Thankfully, Joneira and her band of misfits didn't follow.

Hooking their arms together, Bremusa led her the rest of the way to the docks, the Elder Sea a deep turquoise in the midday sun. "You shouldn't let her get to you, Lina. She's going to be jealous of you no matter how you respond. Her family will want power either way."

Messalina shrugged but kept walking. "It's hard not to. The crown chooses, so her disdain is misplaced. It's not like any of us have a choice in how its favor goes. I don't even want it."

"I know you don't, but it won't matter." Sounds of the busy harbor got louder as they approached where the cobblestone street met the wooden docks. Messalina glanced up, tracking the flurry of movement as ships were loaded and unloaded. "I'll seek the wisdom of the Shadow Glass again, but the crown's choice will be you. What you want won't matter."

Stopping their steps a few feet from the water, Messalina cycled a deep breath, the brine in the sea breeze reminding her of her childhood as she closed her eyes. When she opened her eyes again, the shouts of sailors and the calls of the seagulls flooded her senses again. "Consult the Shadow Glass again, and when you do, tell it to pick someone else."

Messalina and Bremusa spent the rest of the afternoon at the docks, trying the fresh delicacies and ales brought in by vendors from across the realm. The activities at the port were always alluring, the pull of the open sea and the adventures that lay beyond undeniable, at least for someone who'd spent their entire life under the watchful eye of a kingdom. Messalina knew she was being silly, a spoiled princess who had it so much better than so many others, but it didn't bank that fire inside of her, the fire blazing in her heart when there were no fiery wings on her back. Whether the crown chose her or not, she would find herself an adventure.

Chapter Three
Lineage

"Ouch!" Standing on a velvet-covered pedestal, Messalina suffered through a dress fitting, yet one of the many aspects of life in the court.

Glanna, the palace dressmaker, huffed out a breath. "This would go so much quicker if you would just stay still, Milady."

Pulling yet another pin out of the cushion, the female tugged the emerald green corset top of the dress even tighter. "I'd be able to stay still, Glanna, if you'd stop squeezing all the air out of my lungs." Messalina twisted out of the way, the dressmaker nearly toppling off her stool. "And if you'd stop using those things like daggers."

Throwing up her hands, Glanna trudged out of the room as Messalina's older sister, Otera, walked into the bedchamber, her crimson locks standing out brilliantly against her royal blue gown. "You really should give her a break, Lina. She's just doing her job."

Otera crossed the room, sitting on the settee near the window and looking out over the grounds. "Where's Bremusa today?"

Holding up the emerald skirts of her half-made dress, Messalina stepped down from the pedestal and sat next to her sister. "She went into the caves to consult the Shadow Glass." She usually told her sister everything, but she'd yet to tell Otera about what Bremusa had said, about how the crown would choose her, and the daughter she'd yet to have. It wasn't a conversation she was ready to have, not until she knew for sure.

"Will she be back in time for the party tonight?"

It wasn't an answer Messalina had, although she knew her friend wouldn't want to miss it. Neither of them liked the pageantry of the palace, but they still attended its events together, if only for the feasts and plentiful liquor. "Hopefully, but I can't say for sure."

Otera looked away from the window, her blue eyes dark below furrowed brows. "Did something happen at the market yesterday?"

The loud footsteps of Glanna returning echoed through the hallway outside the chamber. Messalina stood, returning to the pedestal. "Joneira and her friends were at the tavern. It was nothing new, just spouting her vile as usual."

The soft click of the door opening signaled the end of their conversation. The dressmaker returned, finished pinning Messalina's gown, and sent her and Otera on their way while she finished sewing their outfits for the night. Their mother and grandmother were already seated for lunch when they entered the queen's apartments in the eastern wing of the palace.

A stately table of mahogany, large enough to seat twenty, sat below a grand chandelier in the center of the room. It was a rather formal setting for just the four of them, but her grandmother, Queen Elowen, was grand in all she did. After nearly one hundred years as the monarch of Aegricia, the crimson-haired queen had grown used to the lifestyle of a royal. Messalina's grandfather, who was her grandmother's consort, however, preferred to spend his time at their farm on the borderlands. She rarely saw him. Since the queen held sole power, he was not needed in the capital for her to rule.

"Ah." Her grandmother's teacup was silent as she set it onto the porcelain saucer. "Join your mother and I for some lunch, my Fires. Sit. Sit." Even with centuries of life behind her eyes, Queen Elowen had barely a sprinkle of silver in her hair. None in their family had been born with phoenix wings, but they all had hair the color of the fiercest flames.

Taking the seat nearest their mother, Messalina grinned as Otera was forced to go around the table and sit closest to their grandmother. Whoever took that seat usually got introduced to a new suitor. Neither of them wanted the queen to set them up on dates, so Messalina was hoping she'd stay off her grandmother's matchmaking schedule, at least for the night. With the number of visitors coming to the palace for the night's party, she wasn't sure sitting across the table would be enough to keep her out of the queen's sights.

"Everything okay with the dress fitting?" their mother asked, her tone much less refined than her mother's. Their mother had been an Aegrician princess for nearly as long as her mother had been queen, but she had always been their mother first. Their mother, Calliope, and their father, Tasos, however, had always remained together, a bonded couple in every sense of the word. Being bonded was everything in their world, mates of the heart and soul, but Tasos fell by an enemy blade in their last skirmish against the barbarian kingdom of Warbotach. Nearly a decade since their father's death hadn't been enough for the pain in Messalina's heart to ebb. She wasn't sure if any amount of time would be. By the look in her mother's eyes as she sat at the table next to the matriarch of their family, Messalina knew her mother felt the same.

Otera nodded, tipping her head as the servant set down two more cups of tea, the steam creating spirals in the air. "Glanna said the dresses should be ready in a few hours."

Lines barely creased her grandmother's face as the queen grinned, clasping lace-gloved hands in front of her. "Lovely. Tonight, is a special occasion so you girls need the best dresses in all the realm."

Messalina inwardly cringed at her grandmother's words. She could only imagine what the special occasion for the party was but was afraid to ask. Fortunately, her sister beat her to it. "Special occasion, Your Grace?" The Queen's smile did not fall as the servant set their lunch on the table, bowls of a rich vegetable stew with pieces of fresh baked bread.

"Yes, my Fires. Tonight, is the night when I announce my intended abdication of the throne."

Her grandmother's intention to leave the throne a year early caught Messalina by surprise. She couldn't blame the queen. After nearly one hundred years of ruling, it would have been time for anyone to seek something different for their lives. What she wasn't ready for, what her grandmother's abdication would mean, was that Bremusa's prophecy could come to pass. If the crown chose her above all others, above her sister... Messalina couldn't even think about that. It wasn't something she wanted, and a year would make no difference.

The idea of going to the party that night and presenting herself to the court as a potential choice for the crown created a tightness in her chest, a need to flee building with every breath. She thought of the ships coming in and out of the port, the freedom setting off on the sea could provide. If the crown chose her to rule, she knew that decision would be made whether she was in the capital or not, but to experience life before that time came… It was more than she could imagine, but she couldn't leave. She couldn't abandon her family or her kingdom.

When Messalina returned to her bedchamber later that afternoon, after leaving the lunch with her grandmother and learning of the queen's intended abdication, Bremusa had still not returned. She knew her friend could take care of herself. As an elemental, Bremusa was more powerful than most people realized, but Messalina still worried about her friend. It was all she could think about as she sat at her vanity and allowed her lady's maid, Elys, to brush and pin her crimson hair.

"Say, Elys." Shifting in her seat, Messalina winced as her attendant snagged a tangle. "Have you seen Lady Aeros today?"

"Not since this morning, Milady."

The palace staff knew more than they were given credit for, but Messalina dropped it. She didn't want to draw attention to her friend's comings and goings, even if she worried what was keeping her. Instead, she sat still, staring at her reflection in the looking glass, while Elys colored the lids of her eyes and placed intricate curls and braids along the sides of her head, a more elaborate hairstyle than she could ever do for herself.

By the time the female left her chambers, Messalina could no longer expand her lungs fully with the emerald corseted dress, and no longer recognized her face with all the makeup. It wasn't who she was. Not really. At least, it wasn't who she wanted to be. She thought about her future, both the future she'd have as queen, and the future she could make for herself if she abandoned her royal title altogether and set out on the continent.

When Otera knocked on her bedchamber door, the sisters intending to walk to the ballroom together, the youngest Lumino sister was still unsure of her decision, but she was out of time. So, with her heart still in a vice, the pressure of a looming prophecy weighing on her shoulders, Messalina rose from behind the looking glass, its reflection not someone she recognized, but someone she needed to pretend to be, at least for the night.

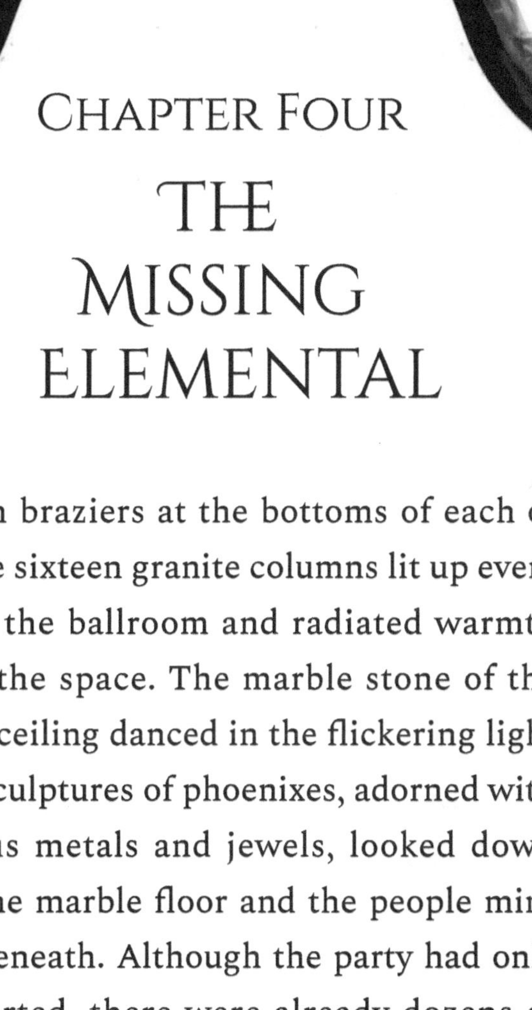

CHAPTER FOUR

THE MISSING ELEMENTAL

Slim braziers at the bottoms of each of the sixteen granite columns lit up every part of the ballroom and radiated warmth across the space. The marble stone of the curved ceiling danced in the flickering light while sculptures of phoenixes, adorned with precious metals and jewels, looked down upon the marble floor and the people mingling beneath. Although the party had only just started, there were already dozens of people in attendance, all dressed in their finest attire. Although the queen intended to announce her upcoming abdication, she hadn't mentioned potential suitors that would be there, but that didn't mean there were none. Without Bremusa by her side,

Messalina had no escape plan for if a male cornered her and asked her to dance.

"What should we do first?" Otera's voice could barely be heard over the music being played by a six-piece band near the back wall of the room.

Messalina leaned forward, speaking close to her sister's ear while scanning the space for their grandmother. She spotted the queen where she expected her, sitting atop her marble throne. "I refuse to walk any further into this space without a whiskey in my hand."

Smirking, Otera held out a gloved hand in front of them, motioning for her sister to lead the way. Messalina didn't have to be asked twice, darting ahead and to the nearest servant holding a tray of glasses, the golden liquid inside flickering like flames in the candlelit backdrop. She had no intention of getting drunk, but she drank one glass quickly to steal her nerves before taking another glass for good measure. Her sister chuckled but sipped her own drink at a much more measured pace. If she needed an escort back to her room that night, she could count on Otera to be that person for her.

"Have you heard from Bremusa?" Concern was clear in the crinkle of Otera's eyebrows. They were both the elemental's friends. "It's not like her to not be back for an event like this."

Her stomach clenching, Messalina shook her head. She'd asked Bremusa to return to the Shadow Glass. If something happened to her friend, she'd be responsible. "I haven't seen her since last night." Messalina set her whiskey glass down on the nearest table, her need to find her friend overpowering her desire to please her grandmother. "I need to find her, Otera. I have a bad feeling about this."

Their mother smiled at them from across the room, the expectation for them to approach and greet the queen clear, but Messalina turned back to her sister, expecting an argument. The sun had already set, and the caves were in the mountains behind the palace. It was not safe to travel anywhere at night, especially not the path Bremusa took. The Shadow Glass was kept in an enchanted place, not somewhere easy to get to, and certainly not a place the two sisters should be visiting on their own.

Taking a glance toward their mother, Otera tipped her head toward one of the warriors acting as a palace guard, a female named Blaedia Solaris. It only took a minute for Blaedia to approach them from across the room, her exotically beautiful face always set in a fierce expression. Messalina remained quiet, waiting to see what was working in her older sister's mind. If anyone had the ability to take charge of a situation, it was her.

The warrior leaned her ear to the older sister, nodding once before leaving the room. Before the shadow of her sword left the room, Otera turned her eyes back on her sister. "Blaedia will gather some of her closest warriors. We'll ride in thirty minutes." Her eyes flicked toward the throne before grimacing.

"We'll need to change, but I'm afraid we'll have to at least speak to our grandmother first. If we run out before giving her an excuse, she'll send the cavalry after us."

The excuse they gave her grandmother was weak: Otera suffering from a mild case of food poisoning and Messalina escorting her back to her chambers. Queen Elowen looked disappointed, and their mother appeared suspicious, but neither argued as they bowed and left the party, neither with a new suitor on their arms.

By the time the sisters changed into tunics and trousers, donned their weapons, and arrived at the servant's entrance, Blaedia was already there, along with three other Aegrician warriors. Messalina didn't know the other females by name, but she knew they could keep them safe. She may have carried a sword and a dagger, but she wasn't nearly trained enough to save herself, much less anyone else. By traveling with the four phoenix warriors not only could they arrive at the caves without taking the chance of traveling on the roads, but with the warriors all having the ability to shift into a phoenix form they could get to the caves quicker as well. They could get there safer.

When they stepped out of the palace and into the moonlit night, the breeze was still, the air too calm, too quiet for the port city. It was unsettling. Messalina loosened a breath and watched as Blaedia and the other three warriors shifted into their phoenix forms with a flash of brilliant fire.

"Messalina, fly with Holera." Her sister pointed to the silver phoenix, her feathers near white in the Moonlight. "We'll fly low, just over the path. If Bremusa is traveling on horseback, or if she's hurt, we'll see her." Climbing onto the back of the beautiful bird, the phoenix near the size of a small horse,

Messalina gripped the reins, but her mind was not settled. There was no way to know if her friend would be traveling in her fae form. Being a shifter, she knew Bremusa could change her appearance, although she'd only ever seen her as the beautiful dark-haired fae female.

The thought of her possibly being injured on the path was something she had to force from her mind immediately. She had to believe that wouldn't be the case. Still, her friend had never been gone for so long without at least sending a raven to let them know she was okay. No matter how much Messalina wanted to believe Bremusa hadn't gotten into any trouble, she couldn't trick her mind into that baseless lie. Until they found her safe and sound, there was no way to know. So, with that pressure adding to the weight already balanced precariously on her shoulders, the phoenixes launched into the air, tendrils of Messalina's hair whipping free from her braid with the force of the ascent.

With Otera astride her back, Blaedia's phoenix form led the way, the bird's feathers mostly black to mimic the onyx hair of her fae form, with her and Holera following closely behind. The other three warriors, whose names she didn't yet know, pulled up the rear. They flew in formation, Holera flying lowest to the road so they could be on the lookout from Bremusa, Blaedia flying slightly higher, and then the other two warriors traveling further out throughout the forest, flying just above the tree canopy.

They passed many travelers, mostly those heading to or from the palace for the party, typically moving by horseback or carriage, but none who looked like Bremusa. Messalina had truly hoped they'd just missed her, and that they'd run into Bremusa along the path, so the further they traveled without seeing her, the tighter the knot in her chest became, until it brought up the burning taste of dread into her throat. All she could think as Holera beat her great silver wings, as the phoenix's violet eyes pierced the darkness, is that they had to find her. They had to find her friend.

It took about an hour to reach the entrance to the caves where the Shadow Glass was kept, and the hum of power protecting it was an unmistakable force, like trying to cross through a wall of quicksand. The phoenixes landed near the entrance, shifting back into their fae forms with the briefest flash of fire, and drawing their weapons before the air chilled in their fires' absence. Blaedia lit a torch before using it to scan the area surrounding the cave, but to no avail. There was no sign of Bremusa, no hint of her having ever been there.

"She's here somewhere," Messalina said, her voice not more than a whisper. They didn't want to draw attention to their location, not from anyone other than who they'd gone there to find.

Blaedia nodded and moved back toward the entrance of the cave, holding the fire aloft to light up the warded space between the outside where they stood and the protected space on the inside where the Shadow Glass stood sentinel over the prophecies of their world.

What Messalina saw when the light illuminated the boundary, the state of her friend and the fear in her friend's eyes, made her fall to her knees.

CHAPTER FIVE

THE SHADOW GLASS

Messalina wasn't sure how it was possible. It shouldn't have been possible, but her eyes did not deceive her. Bremusa, a powerful being in her own right, was chained to the wall of the cavern, but the chains were like none she'd ever seen before. They were black as coal, the power radiating from them unmistakably dark.

"Dragon bone," Bremusa said as she struggled against her bonds to no avail. Messalina darted forward, reaching for the links across her friend's arms but Bremusa huffed out a warning before her hands touched them. "They can only be broken with fire. If you touch them, they'll burn you."

Blaedia stepped forward, flames flicking in her palm. "Who did this to you?"

Holding her breath, her jaw tense as stone, Bremusa remained still as Blaedia held the flame to her bindings. After only a few moments, the warrior had to remove the fire as Bremusa's skin began to redden and blister from the heat.

"Joneira. She's allied herself with a dark witch. They left about an hour ago."

Messalina's blood ran cold. "Why? Why would she do this?"

Clenching her teeth, the chained female nodded for Blaedia to try her flame again. "She was trying to get to the Shadow Glass. She wanted to know who the crown would choose. I was still here when they arrived, and they used the dragon bone to drain my power." The first link in the dragon bone chain fractured under the flame, but Bremusa hissed from the pain so Blaedia pulled away again to give her skin a break. Something in the elemental's eyes flipped and her face snapped toward the warriors. "You need to go back to the palace. They're going to kill the queen!"

A burst of fire was all Messalina saw before two of the warriors shifted and launched into the sky. Blaedia had given them directions, but the whirling in Messalina's mind blocked it all out, everything up until the warriors fled for the capital. "Why?" The desperation in her voice was something she couldn't control, no matter how much pain her friend was in. "Why would they kill the queen? It's not going to make the crown choose her!"

Pulling against her chains again, Bremusa only wore herself out more. When she slumped back against the wall, she was drenched in sweat. "The Shadow Glass prophesied you would be chosen, but that wasn't all it said." Her words trailed off as she scanned the two sisters, clearly unsure if she should say more.

Messalina stiffened, but Otera slid her arm around her sister's waist. "What else did it say, Bremusa?" The elemental dipped her head, holding her swollen arms out for Blaedia to try using the fire again.

"Joneira wanted to know of a way she could take the throne for herself." Hissing through her teeth, Bremusa flinched under the heat of the flames, but didn't pull her arms away as the chain snapped in two, slackening at her sides. "If she kills your grandmother, she can claim the throne, even if the crown doesn't choose her. She won't have control over the portal. She won't even have the power of the crown, but she can still rule. At least by force."

Grabbing Messalina by the arm, Otera pulled her toward the cave's entrance. "We need to go back. We need to stop this."

Blaedia followed behind, but Bremusa stepped away from the wall, holding up her hands to stop them. Her power already funneling back into her, the burns on the female's arms had started to heal. "Messalina, wait. There's more you need to know."

A pit opened in Messalina's stomach at the tone in her friend's voice. It wasn't a tone she'd heard before, but she knew whatever information followed wouldn't be something she wanted to hear. When she turned to face Bremusa, her heart dropped.

Hands still held out in front of her, Bremusa's features were dire. "Messalina, you can't go back to the palace. She knows the crown will choose you. If she wants to take power for herself, she must kill you as well. You need to run. Get as far from the kingdom as you can. At least until it's safe."

For a moment, her world spun. Messalina swayed on her feet, but Otera pulled her tighter to steady her. "I can't just leave, Bremusa. I have nowhere to go." Tears burned at the backs of her eyes, but she wiped them away while she waited for her friend to give her a new option, one she could live with.

Her sister squeezed her tight against her side, rubbing a soothing hand up and down her arm. "There has to be another way, Bremusa. *Any* other way."

The other warrior still stood sentinel by the cave's entrance, silent through everything thus far, a warrior through and through. "Whatever choice is made, Blaedia, needs to be made quickly."

Blaedia nodded once, turning questioning eyes on Otera. Shallow breaths plagued Messalina, the lack of oxygen making her vision blur. Otera loosened a breath. "Is there any other way, Bremusa?"

From the look on her friend's face, Messalina knew the answer before Bremusa spoke it. There was no other way. She had to flee. "The Shadow Glass is never wrong. The only way to keep her safe is to hide her away. The prophecy speaks of a daughter, one that will join the kingdoms as one, one born of Messalina and a human mate. We shouldn't just send her away. She needs to go through the portal, find her mate and bear the future queen. It's the only way to save Aegricia's future."

Knees buckling below her, Messalina fell to the stone cave floor, rocks tearing into her flesh. Her friend knelt beside her, placing a tentative hand on her arm. "I'm sorry I never told you about your mate being human, about your daughter being from another realm. I just..." she hesitated, wiping a tear from Messalina's cheek. "I didn't know how to tell you."

When she looked up at her friend, Bremusa's eyes were glassy. "But you said I would be queen. How was I to be queen, Bremusa? How was I to be queen if I'm to leave our world?"

Her friend shook her head, pain slowing the movement. "The crown will choose you to be queen, Messalina, but it did not say you *would* be queen."

The words made no sense as they met Messalina's ears, but they were still crushing. If she was chosen to be queen, but she was not going to be queen, did that mean...? She couldn't think about it. "Does that mean..." Her words drifted, her eyes closing as she looked away. "Does that mean I must die? Die for the prophecy to come to fruition? For my daughter to save the kingdom?"

Falling to the ground beside her sister, Otera's face dropped into her hands and she shook her head vigorously. "There has to be another way."

Messalina's heart pounded like a war drum between her ears, her body urging her to run, to hide, to be anywhere but where she was. She couldn't die. She just couldn't.

Her friend blew out a slow breath, delicate fingers cupping Messalina's face and tipping it up to look at her. "We won't let it come to that, Messalina. You have my word. You must flee, find your mate, and you must survive. If we can get rid of Joneira before that time comes... The Shadow Glass did not show me your death, only that you would not be queen, although you'll be chosen. We must believe that it will not come to that. But I beg you, please, leave now. *Run. Hide.* Do whatever you have to do to survive. My ravens will find you, and they will let you know when it is time to come home, when it's safe."

Rising to her feet, Bremusa walked to the back of the cave, lifting a satchel from the ground and placing it in Messalina's hands. "Please. Take this and go. I packed this weeks ago, although I hoped I would never need to give it to you. There's clothes, coins, and food, enough to get you started. Follow your heart. We both know it leads you out of this kingdom."

Turning to the other warrior, Blaedia reached out her hand to help Messalina to her feet. "Take her through the portal and leave her somewhere safe. Report back to me. Tell *no one.* Your life depends on this staying a secret."

Bremusa embraced Messalina before Otera took her place, the moment surreal, her mind feeling like it wasn't part of her body any longer. The tears had stopped coming, leaving way for numbness to take over. She knew it would hit her, that she would grieve for everything she lost, but she had to do what Bremusa was asking her to do. The elemental was right, and the Shadow Glass was never wrong. Placing one more kiss on her sister's cheek, and committing Otera's beautiful freckled face to memory, Messalina climbed onto the back of the phoenix warrior, whose name she still did not know, and they launched into the air, heading for the Marella Arch and the human realm beyond.

Chapter Six
Leaving Ekotoria

It didn't take long before the feeling of the sea breeze and the scent of brine in the air met Messalina's senses. It was too dark to see the water below, the moon only illuminating the path directly in front of them, but she knew there was no turning back as they aimed for the portal that would lead them into the human world. She was leaving Ekotoria for the first time in her life, and she was terrified.

The laws made between the two worlds had been in place for centuries. They were not supposed to venture into the human realm, but restrictions or no, they could still physically pass. As an Aegrician warrior, the female on whose back Messalina flew was allowed passage through the portal, a power they were granted in order to protect it. They were given the power to traverse the border, but not to continue into the human lands as travelers, or to seek refuge. If either of them went into the human world and stayed there, they would be violating treaties between the realms, and Messalina couldn't imagine the repercussions for doing so.

Even with the legal challenges to leaving her world, there was more to consider, more complications spinning through her mind as the wind whipped at her hair. Once she left the fae realm, she didn't know how she would survive. How could she protect herself with so little magic of her own? She could glamour her appearance, make the tips of her ears rounded like a human, but there was not much more she had the power to do. Without the wings of fire on her back, the true sign of an Aegrician warrior, she didn't even have the ability to return to Ekotoria on her own. Without a warrior to carry her across, Messalina would be trapped in Inas with no way home.

She was in over her head. The future of her kingdom was weighted on her shoulders and the shoulders of an unknown human mate, a male she didn't even know how to find. Stories in her world claimed the bond was unmistakable, that she would feel drawn to her bonded mate before she even realized the connection between them, but it wasn't something she'd ever experienced for herself to know what to expect. All she could do was hope those rumors were true, and that she wouldn't have to search the human continent for a male who was worlds away and didn't even know she existed. It was all too much pressure on her with the meager energy she had left, so she pushed it all away. Willing her mind to go still, if only for a moment, Messalina laid her head against the silky feathers of the crimson phoenix and fell asleep.

The warbled air of the portal crossing blended perfectly into Messalina's dreamscape, only lulling her deeper into sleep. She did not wake as she entered Inas, but when the phoenix dipped down into the forest and the giant bird's clawed feet landed on the ground, she was finally jostled awake and greeted by another world indeed.

The scent of the majestic pines was a reminder of her home, but the forest she stood in was not one rich with magic. There were no glowing sprites fluttering around, no echo of magic tugging on her own. Vines and flowers exploded among the trees, brightening the space with color where the light of the sun made its way through the dense tree canopy. From where they'd landed, there were no voices of humans nearby, only the skitter of a small creature or the call of a bird. Messalina's pit of loneliness only deepened.

The phoenix shifted as soon as Messalina dismounted, a burst of fire leaving behind a yellow-haired female. "We are near a town, Princess Messalina." The warrior pointed just to the north of where they were standing, although all Messalina could see was trees. "If you keep walking in that direction it shouldn't take you longer than an hour to find an inn and a tavern, somewhere you can rent a room."

Pulling the satchel, she'd taken from Bremusa over her shoulder, hollowness expanded in Messalina's chest. Fear, dread, and the sense of being lost and lonely all mingled in the empty cavity where her heart had been. With a nod, she pulled the hood of her cloak over her head and began walking in the direction of the town, and away from the only link to her homeland, her world, and her family. With every step, the thread connecting her to Aegricia pulled tighter, and she knew it would one day snap. It would break her when it did.

With the sunrise brought the realization of just how different the human realm was from her own. Already, she was beginning to sweat beneath her cloak, the temperature much warmer than in Aegricia, and the lands flatter. Her own kingdom was set deep in the northernmost mountain range of her continent, where snow came for many months per year. She knew there were mountains in the human lands, but she couldn't see them from where she stood. It didn't take long, however, for the path to open before her, leading her into the nearest settlement.

By the time Messalina started to see signs of life, hear voices and the hoofbeats of horses, she could barely keep her eyes open, her heart more awake than the rest of her body. She dug through the satchel at her side, touching the cool metal of the coins before hugging the bag closer to her side. Her sword and bow had never felt so weightless as when she carried everything she owned on her shoulder. When the path through the forest opened to a clearing, sleeping was no longer her biggest priority, and finding her mate was an even more distant goal. Staying safe, not being robbed or violated, that was the most important thing in her life at that moment as she moved toward the wooden door of the Naughty Lyre Tavern.

The name on the sign, in big red letters, made Messalina grin, even though the presence of a pair of males near their horses outside made her grip her cloak around her body tighter. They glanced her way, their conversation halted as she passed, but merely tipped their heads in her direction, resuming readying their saddles after one of them opened the door for her.

With only a few buildings on the main street aside from the tavern, the Naughty Lyre being the only inn, Messalina realized that the town she'd been left near was not a popular place, or at least was not populated. It wasn't a bad thing, however. Less than ten patrons sat inside the space, scattered among the bar and wooden tables, conversing and having their breakfast. The tension in her chest loosened slightly as she approached the bar and sat on one of the many vacant stools, lowering the hood from her head.

A middle-aged human male stood behind the bar, wiping down glasses with a rag. He smiled at her as she took her spot, setting a glass of water down in front of her on the freshly shined wooden surface.

"You must be new to Shefborough, Miss. I haven't seen you here before." A woman, about the same age as the barkeep, flitted around the space, refilling glasses and talking to the customers. His wife, Messalina thought, but she couldn't have been sure. "Can I get a breakfast plate for you?"

She nodded as she took a sip of the water. It was the first drink she'd had in hours. Come to think of it, she hadn't eaten since the lunch she'd had with her family before the party. The familiar pit in her stomach pulsed with the thought of her mother, her sister.

The barkeep set a steaming plate of eggs and grilled meat in front of her, along with a mug of tea, and her stomach rumbled. "Thank you." His smile was genuine, and it may have been because she was famished, but she'd never bitten into such flavorful eggs as those that sat in front of her. "I'm just passing through, but I would like to rent a room, at least for the night."

Just as he was about to respond, the barmaid moved behind the bar, dropping dirty dishes into a bin and winking at the male. When she walked back out into the dining area, he placed a key in front of her. "Room three is open for you, Miss, for as long as you need."

When she slid her hand across the bar, palming the key and pulling it close, it felt like one of the only things she had in the world, at least at that moment. She couldn't stay there indefinitely, but with the number of coins she had she could pay for a room for a while. Before she left for her room, exhaustion weighing her limbs down as much as her eyelids, the barkeep, Tomas, offered to send a food tray up to her that evening if she wanted to enjoy her privacy. The option gave her comfort, a feeling of safety in a world where she needed that more than anything.

Chapter Seven
FANTASIES

With only the key to her room and the satchel over her shoulder, Messalina headed up the set of wooden stairs that took her to the second floor. There weren't many guest rooms in the inn, so the fact that they had any vacancies at all was a small blessing. Even with all the fantasies of leaving her life of obligation behind, never did she see herself with so few belongings, with no anchors holding her to one place or another. Her life in a palace was over.

The guest room was small, but it would be large enough for her uses. The double bed was up against one wall where a large window looked out toward the forest beyond the road. There was also a small table and chest of drawers for clothing. Another small room led out of the bedchamber where there was a small bathing room with a copper tub, toilet, and wash basin.

Dropping her bag onto the table and hanging her cloak on the rack, she first went into the bathing room to freshen up her hygiene. After traveling to the cave in Aegricia and then traveling by phoenix through the portal before having to traverse the forest on foot, Messalina knew she couldn't have smelled that pleasant, so although she was exhausted, she didn't want to get into the bed dirty, not if she wanted to continue sleeping in it. Cleaning up would only take a moment.

Once done, washing her face and body with water from the basin since a bath would have taken too long, Messalina pulled on clean tunic and trousers, leaving her dirty set on the bathroom floor to wash and hang dry later. With her hair still damp, she climbed into the bed, so much less comfortable than her own bed back at the palace, and pulled the blankets to her chin, thoughts of home and everything she lost on her mind as she tried to fall asleep.

Drifting off into the unconsciousness she needed was nearly impossible as she laid below the wool blankets. No matter how much she tried, she couldn't stop the thoughts of her family, Bremusa, her mate, or her kingdom and how it could be facing an overthrow at that very moment. Her grandmother could be dead. The realization had only hit her in that moment, but it only filled her with numbness, and she didn't understand why. Maybe it was because she was too far away for any of it to be real, for it to affect her in any way, or maybe her body was protecting her from the emotions it knew she didn't want to feel.

At some point in the afternoon, as Messalina laid in the bed in the small guest room at the inn, thinking about the family she'd left behind, she'd drifted off into a dreamless sleep. By the time she awoke to a knock at her door, the sun was already descending in the sky outside her windows. Before she had a chance to fall back asleep, to assume the sound had merely come from her own mind, the knock sounded again, startling her.

Sliding off the bed and pulling her cloak onto her shoulders, Messalina crept toward the door, fingers trembling with the thought of answering and it being someone who would make her doubt the fragile safety she'd been trying to create for himself by renting that room.

Thankfully, before she had to make the decision to open the door to whoever stood outside, a mature female voice sounded from the hallway. "It's just me, Miss. Tomas' wife, Deirdre." Messalina breathed a sigh of relief as she unlatched the locking mechanism on the door and opened it to see the same female from the tavern that morning, dressed in a simple dress with an apron, her curly brown hair twisted up and held in place with a quill. A steaming bowl of something that smelled like herby meats and vegetables sat on a tray in her hands. Messalina moved out of the way so Deirdre could enter. "Tomas just sent me upstairs with the meal you requested, Miss. Sorry if I scared you."

The flush came to Messalina's cheeks as soon as she realized how silly she'd been to suspect anything dangerous outside the door. Tomas told her he would send up her dinner so she shouldn't have suspected an enemy. She loosened another breath, a smile spreading across her freckled cheeks. "I'm sorry it took me a moment to answer the door. I had fallen asleep."

Deirdre set the tray down on the small table and waved her hand in front of her. "Unnecessary to apologize to me, Miss. I'm just sorry I woke you. You get all the rest you need while you're here as our guest."

She could certainly see herself doing that if they continued to treat her so hospitably, and if the food this evening was as delicious as her breakfast had been. By the scent of it, it would be. The middle-aged female gave Messalina one more genuine smile before tapping her finger on the table and heading toward the door, Messalina pulling up a chair at the table and calling out after her. "I wanted to thank you and your husband for everything." The female turned around, dipping her head in acknowledgement of Messalina's words. "Oh, and my name is Messalina."

Bowing, Deirdre made her way toward the door, turning to look at her guest one more time before leaving. "It's very nice to meet you, Miss Messalina. And welcome to Shefborough. We're glad to have you. Enjoy your meal." The door clicked quietly as she left the room, leaving Messalina to the fragrant meal and ale on the table and the thoughts of her lonely mind.

Sitting at the table beside the window, Messalina watched as the sun set over the lush forest canopy, the sky turning to pastel shades of pinks, purples, and oranges against the darkening treetops. The stew was outstanding, the cubed potatoes and meaty chunks were well seasoned in the gravy and practically melted in her mouth. She ate the entire contents of the bowl before getting up from her table, the silence of the room starting to get to her.

She'd originally intended to stay in her room all night, rest in the safety and privacy she'd paid for while she could get it, but she was starting to think she wanted more than just silence. There was no way she would run into her fated mate, the destined father to her future daughter and queen of Aegricia, if she just stayed in her room. So, pulling her crimson waves into a braid, Messalina laced up her boots, pulled on her cloak, and left her room to head down to the tavern.

Unlike the morning, when there were only a handful of patrons who were mostly having their breakfast, the night's crowd could be heard as she descended the darkened stairway that opened into the back hall of the tavern. Between the music being played by the small band and the revelry of the customers, it warmed Messalina with a sense of nostalgia, but it made her miss Bremusa even more. They'd spent so much time in the tavern in their own kingdom, drinking Aegrician whiskey and listening to the music, pretending they were not expected to live like royalty.

Now that she thought about it, she wasn't expected to live like royalty in Shefborough either. Just the idea of it felt a bit scandalous, but no one in that tavern knew she was a princess from Ekotoria. She could be anyone in the human lands. As long as she was safe, she could live like a woman of adventure, could *be* a woman of adventure. She could sail the high seas with the pirates or travel the mountains and see faraway kingdoms. She could even fight on a battlefield. The possibilities fluttered through her, nearly giving her wings as the excitement of them lifted her spirits from where they'd been only that morning.

As she moved through the tavern, taking a seat at the one empty table in the nearly full bar, she'd decided that was what she would do. Where she found adventure, she would find her mate, so she would not be afraid to let her heart lead the way to him, wherever it may go.

Chapter Eight
THE HANDSOME OFFICER

The band, composed of four males on stringed instruments and a female singer, played a haunting song about a love lost at sea. Messalina couldn't help but to watch them, a grin on her face, and imagine what their lives must be like, traveling around and doing what they love. It was that same adventure she'd dreamed about when under the thumb of the palace back in Aegricia.

Deirdre approached the table, dropping a mug of ale in front of her and winking before shuffling away, the older female calling out orders to her husband who remained behind the bar. The amber liquor was bitter going down, definitely a different flavor than the Aegrician whiskey she'd grown used to, but it would lighten the pressures weighing down on her all the same. At least, if she did have a few too many glasses of the stuff, she didn't have far to go to find her bed.

Messalina had been strategic in choosing her table, taking one that was far enough from the others to keep her out of notice, but in a location that gave her a good line of sight to watch the music and dancing happening near the stage. Not knowing another soul in the entire realm, she didn't have anyone to talk to, so she chose to just watch the people for a while. It would allow her to understand the humans who she would have to blend in with for the foreseeable future.

A rowdy group of human males sat at one of the larger tables closest to the band, dressed in military-style uniforms with swords strapped to their belts, but tossing back mugs of ale and whiskey as though they were simply revelers. Although she'd only ever seen fae males in Ekotoria, there were certainly some human males that were pleasing to her eyes, so she enjoyed the view as she sipped on her ale, tapping her foot to the music.

One of the men, with dark hair and bright blue eyes, grinned at her over his glass, drawing a blush to her cheeks. He was certainly handsome and looked about the same age as she did. Smiling back, she was still surprised when he rose from his chair and strolled across the room to the table where she was sitting.

"Care for any company?"

The blue of his eyes held her captive as he waited for a response, taking another sip of his drink.

"Okay." Even with all her twenty-two years of life, it was the only word she could utter. Having spent so long under the watchful eye of her grandmother, and with the expectations of the court, flirting and casual dating were never an option, so she didn't know how to act when meeting a handsome male in a tavern. Come to think of it, she had never ventured into a tavern alone. He sat in the chair across from her, movements graceful like a well-trained soldier. His eyes searched hers, waiting for her to say more, but she didn't know what to say. Her mind had gone blank.

"What's your name? Mine is Proteus."

"Messalina."

His eyes seem to light up at her response, the grin on his face genuine and confident. Clearly, he didn't have as hard of a time talking to females as she had talking to males. "That's a beautiful name, *unique*. Are you new to Shefborough or are you passing through?"

Unsure of how much to give away, she grappled with her answer for a moment, before settling on something vague. "I haven't decided yet, but for now, I'm simply passing through."

The band, playing a festive song now, made it difficult for them to hear each other's voices, but he leaned in closer and nodded as she spoke, telling her he was listening above the noise. "As am I. My men and I are on campaign. We will be taking a ship out of southern Vaekros in a few days to go across the continent."

A ship. The first words that came to her mind, the first thought, was of the ships in the Aegrician harbor and how they offered her an escape, an adventure she never imagined she would be able to have with her life being planned out for her. "Would I be allowed to buy passage on your ship?" Eyes lighting, he was quiet for a long moment, making her regret the question. She knew she would've been able to buy passage on a ship in her own world, but she realized at that moment that she didn't know the customs in the human land. Maybe, with that one question, she offered herself up for something she didn't want to give. "I'm just trying to get further from my family. It's a long story, so I'd rather not get into it right now, but if you're going to a place where I could start over, find safety and work, then I would like to buy passage on your ship."

He glanced to the table with his men before turning back to look at her, his eyes soft but his face unreadable. "I don't know you, and I don't need to know your story right now if you don't want to talk about it, but in most cases, it's not safe for a woman to be traveling by themselves, not in most parts of our world. This town is safe, but there are others that are not. If you were looking to get away from this part of the continent, then I would rather you travel with me and my men than chance you get on a ship where the men don't have the best intentions. As a commander of this army, you can travel as my guest. You don't need to pay. I can guarantee you protection while you're with me. These men will not expect anything from you if they know you're my guest, under my protection." Shifting in his seat, he drank what was left in his glass. "Take the night to think about it, interact with my men and get to know us better. Wait to give me your answer in the morning."

She knew Proteus as well as he knew her, but something in his handsome face told her that he meant what he said. She didn't want to be naïve; it was a new world and she was a lone woman traveling without protection, without a family. But if he could offer her safety and get her further away from the portal, then maybe she could find her mate. Maybe she could build a life, give birth to the prophesied future queen, and do what she needed to do to make sure her kingdom was saved when the reign of Joneira was over.

There was the question of whether her people would be able to reach her when her life was no longer in danger, but with Bremusa planning to use ravens to contact her, it shouldn't matter where she was on the continent. Messenger birds enchanted with Bremusa's magic should be able to find her no matter where she was, so all she needed to do until then was to remain untraceable for her enemies, find her mate, and give birth to the kingdom's future queen. It wasn't simple, but she wouldn't be able to do any of it if she were dead.

After Proteus made his offer, Messalina moved to sit closer to him and his men. They were a rowdy bunch, but kind and respectful to not only her, but the other ladies in the tavern. It wasn't a large group, since the other men had remained with their ship, but there had been no warning signs to make her feel that she would be in danger with them. When she thought about it, the entire situation she was in was already dangerous, and being around a bunch of armed men would be safer than being alone in any world.

Proteus kept a watchful eye on her, spending most of the night trying to get to know her, and telling her about himself and his travels. He was the commander of the regiment for the empire's army. The empire had spread to other parts of the continent only recently, therefore his men were being sent to oversee some of those newly acquired outposts. There was no question that there could be danger. He made that very clear. With the far reaches of the continent being newly under the empire's control, there were cases of the conquered people fighting back. The one promise he made to her was that, if she was with him, he wouldn't let anything happen to her.

She may have known very little about human men, Proteus, or the world she found herself in, but something about the way he spoke, about the way he made her feel, told her that he would give his life to ensure that promise was met, to ensure she was safe. So, when the morning came, Messalina packed her few belongings, dressed in a clean set of clothes, and went down to the tavern where he and his men were eating breakfast, and she told him yes. She would travel with him and his regiment as his guest. She would put her trust in the only person in the world that she thought she could and hope with everything she was that it was the right decision.

CHAPTER NINE
FRAGILE REGRET

The group set out a short time after breakfast, leaving the border town of Shefborough behind to travel toward the ship which would take them from the coast of the Vaekrosan empire to the far northern territory of Breqan.

Messalina still didn't know the layout of the continent of Inas, or the empire of Vaekros which bore the colors of Proteus' flag, but she didn't chance asking. If she started asking too many questions about the continent, he would know she wasn't from the human lands, and she wasn't ready to share all her secrets. There was no way for her to explain how she could be in an empire she knew nothing about, so she chose to remain ignorant until she picked up more information through their conversations or caught a glimpse of a map. All she knew for the time being was that she landed near the border town of Shefborough which lay to the northeast of Vaekros proper and was headed northwest to the newly acquired kingdom of Breqan. After landing in Breqan, the regiment would secure the borders and oversee the transition of its local government.

They rode on horseback, Messalina taking up a spot on the front of Proteus' black stallion, Darkflame, as his arms lay wrapped around her, gripping the reins. Although a stranger, something about his muscular body against hers felt right, made her feel safe. Maybe it was because she'd spent her entire life devoid of male affection, but she didn't think that was it, although the fact that he was unmarried and available if she was interested, made the situation a temptation. There was no doubt she was attracted to him, and after their conversation over-flowing liquor the night before, how he always found a way to touch her hand as they spoke, it was clear he was attracted to her as well. She couldn't think too long on it, since she was supposed to be looking for her mate, but she couldn't rule out being with Proteus either. If he could actually be her mate...She couldn't let those hopes fill her to only experience loss again.

"You're deep in thought this morning." Traveling only a few steps away from two other guards and their mounts, Proteus spoke directly into her ear, his warm breath skittering across her cheek and sending shivers down her body. "Are you regretting setting off on the journey? I can return you if—."

"No." Before he could finish the thought, she interrupted him. "I don't regret leaving." She shrugged, smiling at him over her shoulder. "It's just all so sudden, a lot to process."

"I can understand that, and I'm always here to talk about it when you're ready."

"I appreciate that more than you realize. After everything I've given up, it means a lot to have anyone looking out for me."

Taking the reins into one hand, he placed the other atop hers that was resting on the saddle horn. The touch was everything, all her senses zeroing in on that one connection. "I'll look out for you as long as you let me, Messalina."

The feeling of his skin against hers left her breathless. *Speechless.* Certainly, she was wrong, but her mind repeated one word as Proteus' handheld hers. *Mate.*

It was too easy, impossible even, to imagine that the first man she had a conversation within the human world, aside from the bartender at the tavern, could be her mate. Did fate lure the phoenix to carry her to the place where it left her, to the exact place where her mate was traveling? Could it truly be that simple?

Messalina remained quiet for a while as Proteus' handheld hers, as the horse steadily moved forward through the forested hills and plains of the continent. She didn't know what to say. How could she tell this human man, who she'd only just met, that he was hers and she was his? That he was prophesied to be with her so they could give birth to her kingdom's future queen? She couldn't, at least not yet. Without knowing much about humans, Messalina wasn't even sure if they understood the concept of bonded mates, which was so important in her own people. Humans may not have such connections. There was certainly a chance she was wrong, that her heart was trying to convince her of what she wanted so badly, but it was equally possible she was right.

Even if she couldn't tell him, and even if she'd never experienced it before, the longer she sat with her back against his chest, with his hand upon hers, the stronger the draw to him was, until she couldn't bear the thought of pulling away. Everything she'd ever heard about the way a person's body reacts to the proximity of their fated mate was true, and it was something she couldn't deny, even if she couldn't explain it.

The sun made its way across the sky as they traveled, descending toward the horizon as the first scent of saltwater met Messalina's nose.

"It won't be much farther now," Proteus said as his hand stroked hers. She'd never asked him to move it after that first touch hours earlier, and he never offered to, so they'd ridden hand-in-hand for miles, an unspoken understanding that there was something between them, a promise of something more.

"Will we be sleeping on the ship tonight?" The thought made her slightly queasy. "I'm embarrassed to admit this, but I've never even been on a ship."

Proteus chuckled, pointing straight ahead as the rippling waves of the sea appeared just over the crest of the next hill. "We'll sleep on the ship this night and many more." Tucking a strand of crimson hair behind her ear, his smile was warm. "You don't have to be embarrassed about having never been on a ship. That's something many people have yet to experience. I must admit, however, that there's a lot about staying on a ship that isn't pleasant. The movement of the water makes many people ill, and the living spaces are cramped, but the freedom you feel when there's endless blue in every direction, new experiences no matter which way the wind takes you... You can't get that feeling any other way. So, I hope, although you've left so much behind, that you'll find new adventures with me. I hope you never regret leaving."

Regret was such a fragile thing. Even if she regretted leaving her home, there was no other choice to be made. Still, the loss of her family hurt, and the future she could create in the human realm only promised to heal a part of what was missing. "I guess I never thought about the inconveniences of being out to sea. I've thought about leaving my home before, buying passage on a ship and setting sail with the wind at my back, but I'd never had the courage to do it. I know there will always be something missing inside of me, the part of myself that I left back home, but all I can do is try to move on. I can't explain everything right now, but I had to leave for my people. There seemed to be no other way."

He nodded, leaning closer to her and smoothing the horse's sleek black fur. "I'm blown away by your courage. I've known trained soldiers who wouldn't be brave enough to leave their homes like you did, to set out on a whole new life. You may be the bravest person I've ever met, Messalina."

Heat flooded her cheeks at his words, stoking the fire that had already been smoldering with his body so close to hers. "You, kind sir, give me much more credit than I am due. Some wouldn't call me brave for running. They'd call me a coward."

Proteus stiffened, tipping her face toward him with his hand. "Don't ever call yourself a coward. The beautiful blue eyes I see when I look at you are not the eyes of a coward. They're wise beyond their years, passionate and driven. Even though I don't know exactly why you left, your eyes tell me that you left not because you were a coward, but because you felt there was no other choice. You didn't run away..." Messalina's eyes drew closed as his thumb caressed her cheek. "No, Messalina. What I see when I look into your eyes is that your heart and soul are made of wildfire, and you're willing to take on burdens that are not only yours, and carry them solely on your back, to protect those you love. That's what I see when I look at you. You're no coward."

Before Messalina could process the warmth that flowed through her body at his words, Proteus tipped her face toward him, and kissed her.

CHAPTER TEN
CRIMSON FLAGS

The kiss filled her with fire, instantly releasing the tension in her limbs, her body leaning into him for more contact. The kiss had been brief, just a gentle caress of his lips across hers, but it was enough to make her want more. If it hadn't been for the awkward position of their bodies on the back of a moving horse, and the approach of one of his men beside them, she would have pulled him to her lips again.

By the time Messalina turned to look at the yellow-haired male riding on his horse alongside them—Jori, she believed his name was- the harbor had moved much closer, the ship looming in the distance waiting to take them to a faraway land. Surprisingly, it looked no different than the ships in her own world. Crimson flags with three swords through a golden shield emblazoned on their center flapped in the breeze as the craft rocked gently with the rolling waves.

"Should I ride ahead? Ready the men to set off?" he asked Proteus, Messalina's cheeks flushing at knowing he'd seen them kiss. She'd sat near Jori and the other men when they'd been in the tavern, but most of her focus had been on Proteus, so she hadn't had the opportunity to get to know the others.

Proteus gazed toward the ship before turning back to the soldier, nodding his agreement. "Alert the cooks too. I think we can all use something to eat."

With only a brief tip of his head, Jori galloped away on his horse toward the awaiting ship. With them being merely a mile or so away, they would be arriving not long after he did, but she appreciated Proteus' foresight to get things ready for their arrival. She was indeed hungry, exhausted yet excited. The emotions flooding through her were complex, too much for her to process in such a short period of time, but something told her, as the solid wall of Proteus' chest pressed against her back, that no matter how long that process took, he would be there for her in the end. She knew it as true as she knew her own name.

By the time they got to the ship, there was a flurry of activity as men moved along the decks of the craft as well as on the land, all trying to get everything ready for them to set off. There had to have been at least a hundred, although she couldn't have been sure since there were probably more below deck, she couldn't see.

"What made you and a dozen men go inland to Shefborough, while all the others remained behind?" He wasn't obligated to explain the inner workings of his cavalry, or to defend their decisions, but she was curious what had set her fated mate in her path, or at least she believed he was her fated mate from the way her body felt when near him, how her soul seemed to reach out for him even when he was close.

"One of my sailors was injured. There is a proper doctor in Shefborough, so a small group of us set out to bring him to her for treatment."

"Oh, no. Is he okay?"

"He is, although he will not be heading out with us on this voyage. He had to stay behind until he's healed."

The steps of their mount slowed as a young male, no more than a teen, approached them and took the reins, Proteus dismounting only a moment later and reaching his hands up to grasp Messalina's waist and lift her off the animal. He grinned at her as she slid down his body, setting her gently on the ground just as her cheeks warmed, the hue undoubtedly rosy.

Watching as the young man took Darkflame down the path and across the ramp into the ship, Proteus slung Messalina's satchel across his back before hooking his arm in hers and leading her in the same direction as the others had gone. A knot wound in her stomach as they walked, getting tighter the closer they got to the craft that would take her away from where she'd been abandoned and into a future unknown.

The flurry of activity did not slow as Proteus helped Messalina down the ramp and onto the deck of the ship, which was much larger than she'd realized when viewing it from afar. Massive sails were framed by the powder blue sky, no less than ten of them like white sheets billowing in the wind. They took her breath away, along with the realization that she didn't really know what she was doing. It was all part of the adventure, she thought.

After speaking to a few of his men, Proteus placed a hand on the small of her back and led her into the cabin so he could show her to their cabin. Since she was an unexpected guest and the crew was already full, she and Proteus would be forced to share a room, but he offered to sleep on a cot and leave the bed to her. With how she felt when he'd kissed her, she wasn't sure she wanted him to sleep anywhere but with his bare skin against hers.

"We can place our things in the cabin and then I'll bring you to the galley to get a bite to eat," he said as he ushered her down a narrow hallway that had several arched wooden doors on each side. "It would be best to get something in your stomach before we get out into the open water. There, the waves may unsettle your stomach."

She didn't say it, but just the thought of rocking in the waves, with no land to ground her, had her stomach fairly unsettled already. Once they were at the end of the narrow corridor, Proteus opened the last door on the right, which must have been his chambers.

The room was larger than Messalina had expected, with a sizable bed against one wall and a circular table, big enough to seat eight people, in the center of the room. Wooden paneling lined the ceiling, walls, and floors, but there were several windows along one side to bring light into the space. The linens were of a deep blue, like the darkest sea once the sun slumbered. Bookshelves, filled with books and artifacts, lined the wall nearest the door, and another door appeared to lead to a small bathing chamber.

"This is a lot nicer than I'd expected." Stepping a few feet further into the room, Messalina spun in place, taking in the scattered furnishings and decor. Several large maps were rolled up on the table, held in place by some sort of navigation tools made from shiny metal and glass. She took a step in its direction to get a closer look but thought better of it and remained where she was.

"I'm glad it will do, then, since it's our only option." His grin didn't falter as he placed her satchel on the table and returned to her side, reaching out his hand to hers. She stared at it for a moment, knowing if she touched it, she would never let go, but her hesitation only lasted a minute. Only a minute of uncertainty before Messalina forgot about her mate and how he might not be Proteus, at least for that moment, and took his hand, allowing him to slide his arm around her and pull her in close.

When she tucked into his chest, their eyes locked on each other, she could no longer find the words to respond to him, to talk about the room, their journey, or even their lunch. She'd been pulled in, was lost in the cerulean blue of his eyes, not so different from the shade of her own.

"I'd wanted to get my arms around you since I first met you, Messalina, but I didn't know why." Cheeks flushing slightly, he shook his head. "I still don't know why I feel it as strongly as I do." When his eyes dropped to meet her own, they were full of something she couldn't decipher. "Please don't think I'm expecting us to go any further than the kiss on the back of my horse. I do not expect anything from you that you don't want to give or aren't ready to give. I just want to protect you. Okay?"

She nodded, his eyes tracking the movement. "I felt the same way. I—" Hesitating, she bit her lip, her eyes flicking up to meet his stare again. "We need to talk."

CAUTION TO THE WIND

Messalina told Proteus everything. Threw caution to the wind, at least with him. With her family and friends so far away, in a whole other realm, she needed at least one person on her side, one person who knew who she was, and what she was sent to do.

Unsure how he would respond, she was relieved when he didn't immediately reject her when the admission of her being fae fell from her lips, as she relaxed the glamour to reveal the pointed tips of her ears. He didn't discount her words altogether as the ramblings of a mad woman. He believed her, and when she finished pouring her story out, like spilled wine upon the carpet, he reached for her, pulling her against his chest and caressing her back. Eyes drifting shut, she took in his intoxicating scent, what could only be the scent of her mate, and listened to his heartbeat against her ear.

"You've been so quiet." She hesitated, speaking after several quiet moments, eyes opening but staring at nothing in particular as his heart continued to sing to her, the pull of his body undeniable against hers.

Placing a gentle kiss on her temple, Proteus pulled away just enough to look into her eyes and smiled. "I've just been processing. I know it had to have been difficult for you to reveal that to someone, especially someone you've just met, but I'm honored you chose me." Eyes softening, he trailed a finger down her cheek. "I mean that, Messalina. I'll guard your secret with my life."

Warmth spread in her chest, and she knew he meant what he said. "And the prophecy...

What I'm expected to do for my kingdom… It doesn't scare you?"

He pulled her close again, tucking her below his chin. "Nothing about you scares me, Messalina." Kissing her on the side of her face again, he spoke against her hair. "And I can't deny how something innate in me calls to you. There were healers in other towns, but Shefborough was the only place in my mind that day. It's almost liked my soul knew you would be there, knew I needed to find you, to help you." Quieting for a moment, Proteus pulled back to gaze into her eyes. "It wanted me to be with you. I'm convinced of that. So, if the prophecy means to bring us together, then we will be together, and we will be happy."

There were no words to express what she felt at that moment, so she didn't speak. Instead, Messalina lifted herself onto her toes, sliding her hand along the back of Proteus' neck and pulling him to her, his lips to her lips. The surge of their connection was instant, the signal of their bond undeniable. If he wasn't her mate, then her body didn't know it yet.

Everything in Messalina had wanted to allow Proteus to walk her to the bed and claim her as his mate, but they stopped before their kisses moved that far, choosing instead to go to the galley and eat before the ship hit the rough seas. She wanted him badly. Ever since she'd touched him for the first time, her body yearned to get closer, but they had time for that. With all the abrupt changes in her life, and more changes to come, it was best for them to take their time and get to know each other, mates or not. Still, with every touch of their lips, every beat of his heart against hers, there was a promise for more.

By the time they'd grabbed a bowl of stew and a mug of ale and taken their food up to the quarter deck to eat, the land had shrunk into the distance, becoming merely a sliver on the horizon.

Part of Messalina felt like she was leaving behind her past on that land, her family, who she'd been like a distant memory in another life. They ate quietly, so many words on Messalina's tongue needing to be said but none of them finding their way to the surface.

Activity bustled around them, soldiers operating the sails and shuffling about, some cleaning while others arranged the supplies they'd gotten from the port.

Once Messalina and Proteus had taken their last bites of food, their dishes were quickly collected by one of the younger soldiers who then scurried back below the deck. With his hands now free, Proteus slipped his arms around Messalina's waist, pulling her back flush against his chest. She leaned into his warmth, his larger body providing so much more than protection from the cold. His closeness offered her safety as well.

"It's beautiful out here on the water." Messalina's voice was low, barely breaking the silence. "Peaceful."

Proteus smiled against the side of her face, nodding his agreement. "It's easy to lose track of the days here, lose track of where you've been and where you're going, but it is certainly beautiful as the sun sets and rises over the endless blue waters."

Losing track of the days, losing track of where she was going and where she'd come from, it was a scenario Messalina could imagine better than she would've liked to admit. If she were honest with herself, it may have been easier if she could have forgotten where she'd come from, if she could have just pretended her life began on the day, she'd landed in the Vaekrosan forest, on the day she'd met Proteus. Knowing what fate would befall her grandmother, her entire kingdom, but being too far away to remain informed created a constant strain on her heart, her fates pulling her in two directions.

"Do you often run into other ships when on these journeys? Enemies?" She hoped there were no enemies on the seas that could put them in danger, but she knew it would be naive to think otherwise.

Proteus grunted, his strong hand sliding up and down her arm, leaving gooseflesh in its wake. "The sea is a big place. There are certainly dangers out there, pirates and the like, but the flags we fly come with a warning. Any potential attacker would face the full might of the empire if they raised weapons against us, so it is something that is often a deterrent. I'm not saying it can't happen, but it is unlikely."

A small part of her settled at his reassurance. If she could at least be sure of her immediate safety, it was something. With her heart already squeezing in her chest with the nearness of her mate and knowing the setting sun brought them closer to returning to their quarters and the large bed they would sleep in together; any relief was appreciated. She should have been relieved, to find her fated mate so quickly and be able to move forward with ensuring the prophecy came to pass, but she wasn't. She was terrified. To build a life with a male she'd only just met, to even think about becoming a mother, to becoming the mother of the future Aegrician queen, it was a lot to absorb. It was all more than she felt ready for.

They remained above the deck for a bit longer, watching the pastel sky fade to a midnight blue, feeling the cool night breeze die down until the sails were useless to move the ship forward across the glassy water. Soldiers lined the lower deck, gripping the spaced-out oars and rowing them against the sea, the ship resuming its glide into the darkness. With the extra bodies on the deck, and the noise and movement they brought with them to guide the ship, Proteus took Messalina by the hand and led her back to their quarters, to where they could find quiet and warmth in their private room.

The moment the closing door made a soft click, leaving them alone once again, Messalina sucked in a deep breath as Proteus turned to face her, sliding his arm around her waist. He would never expect more from her than what she was ready to give. She didn't know him well, but she knew that to be true. What she also knew, as he pulled her close and pressed his lips against hers, sliding his tongue across the seam of her mouth, tempting her to open for him, was that she wanted more, she wanted all of him. They may have had a future to plan for, and a future they could fill with intimate moments once they got to know each other better, and they would do exactly that, but they wouldn't wait any longer to claim each other as mates, not if it was her decision to make. There wasn't much about her life she knew, not anymore, but she knew she wanted him to become hers in every way, and she intended to show him exactly what she wanted that night, if he would let her.

CHAPTER TWELVE

IT'S OKAY TO SAY NEVER

When Proteus threaded his fingers into Messalina's hair, tilting her head as his tongue slid along the seam of her lips, the taste of him sent urges through her body that she didn't think she could fight. She didn't know where she was going to end up, but she knew wherever it was, it would be with him, and that was all she needed to know.

His kisses were slow, cherishing, a heart-squeezing gentleness she would've never expected from a career soldier. In front of his men, he had the confidence of a leader, stern but warm. With her, he was tender, hopeful but unsure. He'd never assumed she would be his, never insisted she make a decision. Instead, he showed her care and affection, and left the rest in her hands.

Lifting her in the air, Messalina's legs went around Proteus' waist as he walked her to the bed, their lips never leaving one another. She'd kissed males before, albeit not many, but none had ever felt like this. Maybe it was because she was lonely, desperate for someone to replace the family she'd left behind, but she didn't care. It felt right and that was all that mattered at that moment.

When he set her on the bed, he pulled away, Messalina left panting as she searched his face. "We don't have to do this, Messalina. We can wait." Responses flooded her mind, but she didn't say anything for a moment, her heart beating too wildly to verbalize what was in her head. He paused, sitting beside her and taking her hand in his. "I don't want you to do something just because of the words of a prophecy. That's too much pressure on anyone."

When she looked up at him through her lashes, she couldn't miss the sincerity on his face and it warmed some deep-down part of her, but she wasn't doing it because the prophecy told her to. *Not really.* She wanted to be sure he was her mate. That couldn't be denied, but she also wanted him, wanted something in her life that would bring her happiness and contentment when everything else had been ripped away. Maybe she was rushing, but in the grand scheme of things, why not?

It was the one question she came back to when she leaned forward and placed her lips on his again, Proteus kissing her back with a renewed vigor. "I'm not trying to be with you because of the prophecy." Her words came out breathy as she pulled away to look him in the eyes. "There are many reasons why I want to be with you right now, and I'm sure there are a few reasons why I shouldn't, but none of them are because I think I have no choice."

When his eyes searched her face again, he seemed to realize she was telling the truth.

All she could think of was how handsome he was. She'd never thought she'd end up mated to a human man, not that it was ever an option. There were no humans in her own world.

His arm slid around her, gently guiding her back on the bed as he crawled over her. Even with her permission, he wasn't rushing anything, and she appreciated that. It was like they had all the time in the world, even if they didn't. Once they made it to land, to the newly acquired Vaekrosan outpost, Proteus would have to do his job, which may put him in danger. Messalina didn't know what her place would be in that new world, but she was curious to find out.

Proteus' rose to his knees between her thighs, untying his tunic and tossing it to the side, his blue eyes never leaving her, his muscular chest moving with his breaths. "Are you sure, love? It's okay to say no." Pausing for a moment, he leaned forward, placing a hand on her knee. There was so much question in his eyes, so much longing. "It's okay to say never."

Instead of responding, Messalina reached for the hand that was on her knee, sliding it up to the ties on her tunic. His eyes were wide, his nostrils flaring, as he watched the movement, but he didn't pull his hand away. She left her hand on his for a moment, unable to get enough of the feeling of his skin against hers. When she did pull her hand away, sliding her fingers into his hair, he began unlacing her ties, expertly working his way down the front of her tunic as his mouth claimed hers once more.

The ship swayed as it moved through the sea, sounds of wood creaking and waves colliding with the craft blending with the sounds of their breaths. Helping her to remove her tunic, Proteus tossed it to the side before his callused hand returned to her stomach and slid it gently up to her breast.

The touch was like lightning, her back arching off the bed as it sent tingles through her body. Proteus nuzzled into her neck, swirling his tongue on the sensitive flesh as his hand explored her curves.

"Stunning," he whispered in her ear, the warmth of it only stoking the fire burning inside of her. If there had been any doubt before, it had vanished. Even if the prophecy had never been spoken, her body yearned for release. It yearned for him.

"So are you." The rasp in Messalina's voice surprised even her. Proteus huffed a chuckle as he kissed along her collarbone.

"Thank you." He didn't lift his lips from her skin as he spoke, the vibration of it making her giggle.

"What? It's true." The words died in her throat as Proteus traced the peak of her breast with his tongue, taking it into his mouth.

Her eyes fell shut, every swipe of his tongue on her nipple making her bite her lip harder. Needing so much more, she reached between them, cupping the hardness through his pants as he lifted to kiss her again. Unlike their earlier kisses, that were passionate yet languid, tender, this kiss was claiming.

He groaned against her lips as she stroked the impressive length through the fabric of his pants. "Are you sure you want to do this, love?" Breaths coming out in shallow pants, Proteus' eyes gazed into hers, waiting for her choice. It *was* her choice, after all. She nodded, leaning up to suck his bottom lip into her mouth as her hands fumbled with the clasp of his pants.

Unable to work the clasp, Messalina gave up as his hands took over, unbuckling his pants while they watched each other. Just as he was beginning to shove them down his hips, someone knocked on the door.

Proteus' shoulders stiffened and they held their breaths, waiting to see if the knock would repeat itself. To Messalina's dismay, it did, several more times. Huffing out a breath, he pulled his pants back up, refastening the buckle as he climbed off the bed. Messalina quickly laced her tunic, climbing off the bed behind him.

The knocking became more insistent as he pulled his tunic from the floor and over his head. "Alright. Alright. I'm coming." He glanced back at her, a crooked grin on his face, before grabbing the handle of the door and slipping outside, leaving her with her thoughts and a craving only he could satisfy.

CHAPTER THIRTEEN
PIRATES

Proteus had only been gone for a moment before he darted back into the room, reaching for his sword. "I need you to stay here. Lock the door behind me."

Messalina's heart fell into her stomach at his tone. She reached for her own sword, pulling it over her shoulder. "Proteus, what's wrong?"

Pausing as he was putting on his boots, he glanced up at her under heavy brows. "There's a ship. *Pirates.* They haven't done anything yet, but they're closing in on us." Tightening his laces, Proteus stood and straightened out his weapons belt. "I don't want you in danger. You'd be safest down here. I won't be gone long."

There was a part of her that wanted to listen to him, to hide and let others fight, but she was an Aegrician. She'd always wanted to be a warrior, and now was her chance. Reaching for his arm, she steadied her voice. "I'm not going to hide while the rest of you fight. I've been trained with a sword, a bow. I can help."

He didn't want her to go. She could see it in his eyes, but he only took a moment to nod. Only once, but it was enough. When he stood, he took her hand, and they left the room together.

They hadn't even gotten to the end of the hall before the first shot was fired, the cannon shaking the entire craft. Messalina's hands flew protectively over her ears as Proteus held onto her, pulling her into his side. "It's okay. It's okay. I've got you. That was our cannon, not theirs."

She nodded, but his words didn't make her feel any better. If they'd shot at the pirates, that meant the pirates could shoot at them.

When they started walking forward again, Messalina was trembling.

When they walked out onto the main deck, there was chaos, at least from Messalina's point of view. Dozens of men stood on one side of the ship, preparing the cannons and working the sails. Just over the heads of the soldiers, she could see the other ship's sails, solid black with red bones crossed at the center of each. It was smaller than the ship they were on, but only just.

Another cannon boomed, nearly knocking Messalina off her feet. Proteus wrapped his arm protectively around her as they shuffled toward where the captain stood behind the wheel. "Miron." Proteus had to speak loudly over the shouting on the deck. One of the men near the captain stepped forward, an older male with graying hair and a long beard of the same color. "Look after Messalina." Letting go of her hand, he went to walk away but she reached for him, grasping his wrist. When he turned back to her, his face was more serious than she'd ever seen it. "I need you to stay here while I go talk to my men, love. If you're by my side, you'll be all I think about." He pulled her in close, kissing her fiercely. "You'll be all I think about no matter what. Just please," he said again, kissing her hand before letting it go. "Stay here until I return."

Before she could respond, before she could reach for him and beg him to take her with him, he'd darted off and into the crowd of soldiers.

"Here you go, miss." Miron reached for her, trying to get her attention, but she didn't turn right away, still watching the direction in which her mate had disappeared. When she reluctantly turned away, Miron's hand was still held aloft. "You can sit here, miss," he said, guiding her to a bench nearby but she shook her head, needing to stand, needing to feel helpful.

"No. I need to be ready to fight." Whatever he'd heard in her voice, he didn't argue, only nodded and stepped to her side, hand on the hilt of his sword.

They watched as the pirate ship moved closer, the first cannon erupting out the side of the black-flagged ship and nearly missing their own. Messalina's heart sat in her throat, the violent beating making her sick. Their own cannon fired again, taking off a chunk of the pirate ship's rear.

Just as she watched the chunks of debris fall into the sea, she could just barely make out the small boat slide out from around the other ship's shadow. Several men sat in the small vessel, rowing in a steady beat toward them. It would be a silent attack, if they managed to remain unnoticed. Messalina knew her own vision in the dark was better than that of humans, so she was not going to chance the boat closing in.

She took a step to leave, but Miron's arm shot out to grab her wrist, his eyes pleading with her to stay put. It had gotten too loud to hear each other speak, the sound of shouts and cannon fire filling the air. Shooting him a glare, refusing to be held back, she wrenched her wrist out of his grip and ran forward, in the direction of her mate.

Messalina searched the faces, bracing her feet when the cannon erupted again before continuing to move. Unable to find him anywhere among the other men, she told anyone she could about the encroaching row boats before darting back below deck and toward their shared quarters. She wasn't going to hide, however. She was going for her bow.

Below deck was chaos, cooks and those who were not soldiers trying to find a safe place to hide. She moved past them in a hurry, nearly tripping over one of the teen boys running into one of the closets. "Sorry!" she yelled, continuing before he had a chance to even notice who'd collided with him.

Throwing the door open, it only took her a moment to grab her bow and quiver of arrows and race back the way she'd come in. She was back on the deck in only a few minutes, yet the activity had only gotten more chaotic.

Stopping on the deck, she searched the faces of the men again, looking for Proteus, but couldn't find him in the crowd. She couldn't stand there and wait for him. There was too much going on, too much at stake. Giving one more cursory glance toward the men moving about the deck, Messalina turned and headed for a higher viewpoint.

Darting toward the bow, Messalina took a ladder to the highest point, planting her feet beside another soldier. He gave her an incredulous look, but returned the binoculars to his eyes, yelling out instructions to the men below. She scanned the water, bile rising in her throat when she saw that there was no longer only one small boat of men rowing toward them. It had become ten times that. Pulling an arrow from her quiver, she aimed her bow, taking aim at the boat closest to them.

Firing, Messalina swore as the arrow narrowly missed one of the men holding an oar in the closest rowboat. She was undeterred, pulling free another arrow and nocking it in place. When she shot the second time, she met her mark, hitting him in the chest. The man fell over, his oar landing in the water.

"I don't know who you are, miss," the man next to her said, "but that was impressive."

She couldn't help but to grin as she pulled another bow out of the quiver. He'd already gone back to doing his job. "Thanks."

Messalina fired three more arrows before the first of the pirates climbed onto the deck, intermixing with the Vaekrosan soldiers ready for their arrival. Heart hammering in her chest, she watched as fighting ensued, the clang of metal against metal filling the night air as she took shot after shot, downing as many men in paddle boats as she could.

The arrows did not last, her quiver not holding enough to last for the duration of the fight. Upon firing her last one, Messalina tossed her bow back over her shoulder, nodding at the man by her side before climbing down the ladder to help in the fight.

Once she got back down to the main deck, Messalina scanned the faces again, desperate to find Proteus. She needed to know he was okay, but she didn't see him, and she couldn't wait. Instead, she drew her sword, and swung it at the first pirate she saw, warm blood splashing across her tunic as she caught him in the neck. The last thing she saw, before his head hit the ground, was his eyes widened when he realized he was going to die at her hands.

The battle was a chaotic scene, Messalina slashing her way through the deck, making sure to strike only the enemy as she looked for her mate. Before she realized it was over, the last enemy fell at her feet, and a strong arm slipped around her waist, her body jolting as her arm pulled back to strike.

"It's me! It's me, love." Proteus' blue eyes caught hers, his face streaked with blood. "It's over."

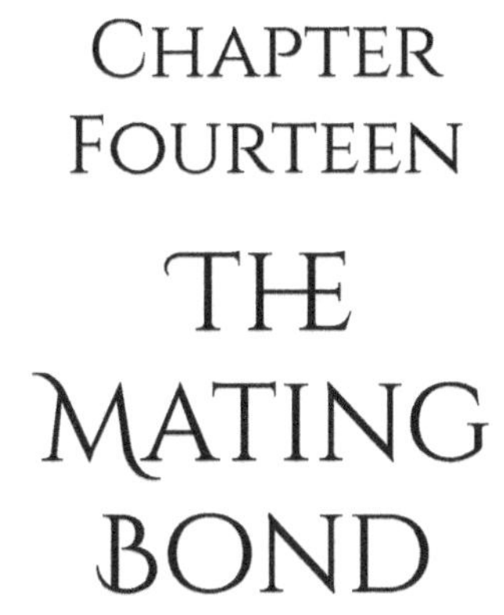

Chapter Fourteen
The Mating Bond

I t took a moment for Messalina's mind to catch up with what Proteus was saying, her adrenaline still pumping ferociously through her veins as she searched for the next enemy to strike. When she realized what he was saying was true, that it was truly over, she slumped into his arms and let out a deep breath, her sword falling to her feet.

"You're okay, love." Proteus ran his hands down her back, turning her in his arms and leading her away from the carnage. "Let's get you cleaned off. It's all over."

There was still so much activity on the deck behind them, wails of the injured and bodies that needed to be disposed of, but Proteus led her below deck anyway, and to the safety of their shared chambers. In all her life in Ekotoria, she'd never experienced anything even close to a battle. She'd never killed another person before tonight, and his eyes still lingered in her mind. When the door of their chambers clicked shut, Messalina's legs crumbled beneath her and she fell to her knees.

Sitting on the floor next to her, Proteus pulled her onto his lap, nuzzling into her hair. She remained quiet for a few moments, breathing deeply to calm her mind as his lips on her neck sent shivers across her body. "If you're intending to distract me, Proteus, I'd like to bathe first."

She felt him chuckle against her skin before he pulled away, looking down at his own gore-covered clothing. "I think we both need to take a bath before we go any further, actually."

Rising onto his legs and reaching down for her, Proteus led Messalina into the private bathing room, guiding her to sit on the stool near the tub as he filled the tub, adding hot water from above the fire. She watched him as he untied his bloody tunic, dropping it to the ground and leaving his muscular chest bare. He truly was built like a warrior, his body sculpted from wielding a sword. With his pants riding low on his hips, it took everything in her to look anywhere but where the muscles of his abdomen rippled below his waistband. She bit her lip, her hands itching to touch him as he reached for her, pulling her to her feet.

"May I?" he asked as he let the top tie of her dirty tunic wrap around his finger, the movement drawing her attention and she wanted him to pull, to remove her tunic and touch her.

She nodded, lifting her eyes to meet his. Everything they'd gone through in the past hour fled from her mind as she got taken by the depthless blue in his gaze. "Please." Her response was merely a whisper, but it was enough. His fingers worked slowly through each lace of her tunic, the tension of the moment feeding the building passion inside her. They'd come so close to being together before they'd been attacked, and she hadn't forgotten how badly she'd wanted him. Sliding her hands up his sculpted chest, Messalina leaned forward, her lips hungry for him as she kissed him.

Sliding her hands down to the waistband of his pants, she fumbled nervously with the buckle, Proteus taking over after only a moment and sliding them to the floor. Their lips never left each other, his tongue sliding against hers in a dance she could feel all the way to her core. He pulled away, his eyes asking permission as gentle fingers guided her tunic over her shoulders and onto the floor.

They looked at each other for a moment, his hardness pressing against the fabric of his undershorts, her breasts heaving with breath beneath her breast band. Proteus licked his lips, his finger tracing along her collarbone. "I need to get you in the bath before the water cools."

She nodded, unclasping her breast band as he kissed her again. Her trousers fell to the floor a moment later, her mate's lips leaving hers as he helped her into the bath, the steaming water a luxury after the long ride on horseback and the battle. The tub wasn't large, not that one could expect much more in such a small space, but he removed his undershorts and climbed in behind her, her back sliding in between his thighs as he held her.

"You were amazing out there, Messalina." Reaching for a copper mug beside the tub, Proteus filled it with warm water and poured it over her filthy hair before lathering it with a lavender scented shampoo. "Thank you for all you did to help us. You are truly remarkable."

Although she tried to suppress the blush, she felt her cheeks warm at his words. "Thank you." She hesitated, closing her eyes as the water rinsed over her hair and down her chest. "I truly had no idea what I was doing. I'd never been in a situation like that before. In my own kingdom, I would have never been allowed to be a warrior."

Proteus huffed, wiping her forehead with a cloth. "I'm not sure what it takes to be a warrior in your kingdom, but you are certainly worthy of one."

It had always been what she'd wanted, to have been born with wings of fire, with the ability to shift into a phoenix and soar through the clouds. Thoughts of her homeland, her family, lined her heart in sadness and she quieted for a moment, willing it to pass. Her focus needed to be on her future. It was what was necessary to save her kingdom, after all.

They finished bathing after that, the stressful activities of the day begging Messalina's eyelids to close. She didn't want to sleep, not at all. What she wanted was to crawl into bed with her mate and feel his skin against hers. When he guided her out of the water, pulling her into his arms as he wrapped a large towel around her, she realized he wanted the same thing.

Sliding one arm around her back and the other beneath her knees, Proteus lifted her, carrying her out of the bathing room and into the bedchamber, setting her down on the bed. It was impossible for her to ignore his hardness that was filled with passion and pressing against the towel wrapped around his waist. Her body yearned for him as she slid back on the bed, the towel sliding off her body with the movement.

He stood still beside the bed, watching her with a hunger she knew was reflected in her own face. Slipping below the blankets, Messalina lifted them in invitation, her bare body all that remained once the towel had been pushed aside. His nostrils flared and he crawled in on top of her, his lips meeting hers again, the warmth of his skin sending heat through her body.

Reaching her hand between them, she tugged at the towel around his waist, pulling it aside in one try. Proteus chuckled, the sound silenced as she kissed him again, pulling his bottom lip into her mouth.

His groan reverberated deep in her belly as he ground against her, his hard length lining up perfectly with the most sensitive spots of her. Just one movement and they would be joined as one, but he refrained, slicking himself in her wetness as he trailed his mouth down her neck, her chest. "We can still wait, Messalina."

The warm breath against her skin threatened to drive her over the edge and she wrapped her legs around his waist, desperate for more friction. "No." She ground against him again, hissing as his cock rubbed against her center. "I don't want to wait."

He nodded, continuing to kiss his way across her collar, her breasts, every touch like lightning against her skin. Her body bowed off the bed as he slid down her, his mouth tracing the planes of her stomach as his hands caressed her breasts. A breathy moan escaped her as she slipped her fingers into his still damp hair, tugging lightly on it as he moved further down until he rested between her thighs.

The first caress of his tongue against the sensitive bundle of nerves between her legs had her back arching off the bed again, her gasp loud enough to be heard down the hall. It only encouraged him, and he licked her again, groaning under his breath as he devoured her, the feeling like nothing she'd ever experienced. Proteus was her mate, no matter what the prophecy predicted. Being with him at this moment, there was no way she could imagine being with anyone else. It just wasn't an option. Her body knew.

The coil deep inside her belly wound tighter with every stroke of his tongue, his hands, until he brought her over the edge, her climax crashing over her like the waves against the bow of the ship. Her body stiffened, her thighs holding him in place as she rode the wave of pleasure, his name on her lips. When it was all over, her body went limp, and he kissed her on the thigh, climbing over her once again.

Reaching between them, Messalina took his hardened length in her hand, desperate to touch him, to have him inside her. Proteus groaned, his cock slick with her release as she guided him to her entrance. His eyes searched hers, but he didn't ask her for permission again, because she'd made her choice as she wrapped her legs around his waist, pulling him to where she wanted him. There was no question about what either of them wanted, and she didn't intend to wait anymore.

The first stroke of Proteus inside Messalina filled her with heat, liquid fire flooding her veins. A moan ripped out of her, but it was silenced as his lips took her again, every thrust sending her body closer to the edge. Her nails dug into the corded muscle of his back as Proteus gripped her hips, holding her in place as he filled her with every stroke.

Moans turned to screams against his lips as Messalina crested over the edge again, her insides gripping him as he went with her.

There was no question in her mind, as Messalina laid in Proteus' arms, both dripping with sweat and panting, that he was meant to be her mate. She'd laid with a male before, had been driven to the edge with pleasure, but none ever made her feel the way he had. He was the one she'd been meant to find. Closing her eyes, she luxuriated in the feel of his skin against hers as he traced idle shapes on her stomach with his fingers until they fell asleep in each other's arms.

If you plan to continue with this series, there's an epilogue...but I suggest you stop here if you don't like cliffhangers and don't plan to continue.

Thanks for reading!

Chapter
Fifteen

EPILOGUE
For Aegricia

Climbing onto the main deck, Messalina pulled in a deep breath, the crisp sea breeze filling her lungs. Proteus stood behind her; his strong arms wrapped lovingly around her waist. They'd spent weeks living on the ship with his men, Messalina doing odd jobs as Proteus trained with his men during the day and growing close as mates and lovers at night. After only seeing the endless blue of the sea for so long, Messalina was filled with excitement when land appeared on the horizon.

She pointed, Proteus nodding before kissing her on the cheek. "We are almost there, my love. Are you ready to set off on a new adventure with me?"

Ever since leaving Ekotoria, her life had been one nonstop adventure and she smiled every morning when she woke up in his arms. As she watched the continent moving steadily closer, her heart was filled with hope. "I look forward to adventure with you, but to settling down somewhere safe even more so." She hesitated, turning around to face him. "Somewhere we can build our future."

Smiling, Proteus leaned forward and pressed his lips to hers, the kiss full of promise. "No matter where we go, Messalina, I will keep you safe." He kissed her again, his lips lingering as he slid his arms around her waist and pulled her closer. "And no matter where we go, we will be building our future."

Laying her cheek against his uniformed chest, she nodded as the breeze whipped at her crimson hair, the strands like fire in the sun. They would, indeed, build that life together, for each other, and for the kingdom of Aegricia.

That thought was the one thing that kept Messalina awake at night, especially after she'd received the raven that spoke of her grandmother's death, was what kind of future they could build. Joneira had seized power by force. Otera and her mother were in hiding. As she watched the land approach, and the promise it offered her own life, she could no longer fool herself into thinking the prophecy would not weigh on her decisions. Until she fulfilled her obligations to her kingdom and returned to see the crown resting on the head of its rightful ruler, she would always be shadowed by the prophecy spoken by the Shadow Glass. Still, Aegricia was a world away, so she held her mate and made a promise to herself that they would build their future together, and in that future, she would find a way to save her people.

To be continued...

ENJOYED SHADOWED BY PROPHECY?

Enjoyed Shadowed by Prophecy? Please leave a review!

You can also check out the entire Crown of the Phoenix series and its other prequels here!

https://www.amazon.com/dp/B0B258Y1SD

C.A. VARIAN

THE OTHER WORLD

SAMPLE

THE OTHER WORLD SERIES

BOOK ONE

CHAPTER 1
ELIANNA

"**S**ome say the worst thing about having cancer is knowing you have cancer, but I'd say the worst thing about having cancer is throwing up my perfectly good pizza because of the meds."

A few people in the group circle nodded, voicing their agreement before Elianna continued. "My name is Elianna Foster. I'm nineteen years old and I have stage IV thyroid cancer that's invaded my lungs like Battlestar Galactica."

The entire group, twenty people sitting in a circle, called out "Hi, Elianna" in unison, some giggling at her nerdy comment.

She bowed from the waist and sat back down, stifling a cough and securing her oxygen cannula in her nose. The one thing she didn't say out loud was that she wasn't going to get out of the disease alive. She didn't have to say it. Everyone at that meeting had some form of cancer. All of their lives were on borrowed time.

"Are you going to use the key?" asked one of the younger men in the circle.

She believed his name was Liam, but she couldn't have been sure. From hearing his conversations with the others, all she knew was that he had leukemia and was sixteen years old. It wasn't often she got close to anyone from the circle of the sick. She didn't want to go through the heartbreak of losing them. Elianna's swaggering, nonchalant facade almost fractured when asked about the controversial key, but she fixed her face quickly, securing her walls back into place.

The Keys of Ecromos were the only way to open the portal in the Shrine of Solstice and cross into the realm of the fae, but keys weren't given to just anyone. For a human to cross, they had to be female, had to be dying, had to be left with little hope for their lives in the human realm. If it was a matter of survival, women who crossed over into the realm of the fae would be relieved to be there, glad even, and wouldn't fight what was expected of them. They wouldn't fight to return home. The hopelessness that was necessary to make that choice, at least for Elianna, made it an impossible decision.

According to the stories, it was rare for fae females to bear offspring, a genetic mutation that was causing the race to die out. Fae healers could cure human diseases, but the infertility among their females was something they couldn't fix. On top of this already devastating issue, most of the children born to fae couples, if the child even survived, were male.

Elianna didn't know much about Ecromos, aside from the rumors, but it certainly sounded like the fae needed to breed with humans before their people, and the magic they held, died out for good. She was empathetic to their plight, but she was also only nineteen years old, and had no interest in settling down and having children, even if she wouldn't have to leave her world to do it.

Aside from the rumors and legends, the portal was a mystery to the humans, as was the world beyond it. Since no one came back out, there was only speculation as to what met those who entered. The door into Ecromos only allowed travel in one direction. Some said the human women were used like cattle, breeding half-fae children for the wealthy, but others speculated the key given to each human woman was matched to a single fae male, their fated mate, and that he would be waiting for her when she crossed over.

The idea of a soulmate was a much easier idea to swallow than the worst case scenarios that plagued Elianna's mind, but it was still a reality she wasn't yet ready for. She wasn't sure if she'd ever be ready to be a wife, or a mother. The question was not whether she was ready, but whether being forced to have children with a male she didn't know was better than death.

Either way, Elianna hadn't yet decided what she would do if the time came where she would be forced to make the decision to leave her home, or die. With the cancer in her lungs making it so hard to breathe, she knew she would have to make a choice soon. *Ready or not.*

The fae could cure her cancer and give her a near immortal lifespan, but they wouldn't take her once she was too far gone. When she reached the point where only machines could keep her alive, it would be too late. She had to make a decision- *soon.*

Forcing her face back into something less melancholy, Elianna cleared her throat. "I haven't decided if I'll use the key. I know it's unlikely I'll beat this thing, but we also don't really know what's through that door. And once you cross, you can't come back." She smirked, faking a confidence she didn't feel. "I don't know if I'm ready for that level of commitment. Never been much on commitment anyway."

A few people laughed, but there were some who didn't, making her regret the joke.

She didn't know the middle-aged woman who stood, but the grimace she wore made the woman's lack of amusement clear. Elianna shriveled back inwardly, even if her face didn't give away her discomfort. "At least you have that option. Women my age have no option but to die. There are no keys being offered to us. No chance at hope. If there were, I'd gladly take it. Maybe you should think about that before scoffing at your one chance to live."

Elianna left the cancer support group feeling less than stellar. Using the key was a very personal decision. She realized that. But the woman's comments still stung, still made her feel like she was being a spoiled child. Maybe that's what she was, but she was only nineteen years old, so was she really expected to see the decision as anything more than an overwhelming burden?

Even with all the unknowns, the possibility to survive her fate, to be healed, was alluring. Maybe the woman from her group was right, but Elianna wasn't there yet. The current treatments weren't going to cure her, but they were holding the Grim Reaper at bay.

Tapping her hands on the steering wheel of her red sedan, she listened to the radio, willing the stranger's words out of her mind.

Elianna's mother, Elizabeth, was already setting dinner on the table by the time she arrived back home to the city of Brookwood. Her family hadn't always sat at the table to eat dinner together, but her mother insisted on it ever since Elianna's cancer had spread to her lungs. From that point on, she was made to sit at the kitchen table every night, listening to her father talk about his clients, and her mother talk about only the gods knew what. She loved her parents, but it was as boring as watching the television on static. She suffered through it anyway. Her parents would miss her when she was gone, so sitting through family dinners every night was a small price to pay. They were great parents. They loved and took care of her through it all, so she would have given them anything she could while she was still there to do so.

Her mother smiled when she walked in, her blue eyes always bright, even with the shadow of grief behind them.

"How was group?"

Shrugging, Elianna grabbed a buttered roll before plopping into a chair at the table. The woman's comments hadn't helped the nausea that always plagued her, but she was determined to eat anyway. "Same as always.

Aside from Jerry dying, the conversations don't really change."

Her mother stopped laying out food and looked up as her father, Peter, walked in and sat at the table before responding. "Is anyone planning to use a key?"

"Mom." Elianna mustered as much annoyance in her tone as she could.

It seemed the repeated conversations would continue at home as well. The way she would constantly bring up the subject of the key, it was almost as though her mother had given up hope on her. Once she used the key, her chance of staying with her family was gone. She wasn't ready to give up just yet, even if her mom seemed to be. Was ending up enslaved any better than death? She didn't have all the answers about what took place on the other side of that door, but becoming a sex slave, or no more than a breeding animal, were two very real possibilities. She wasn't sure if either of those were better than the alternative.

Her mother put her hands up in supplication. "Alright. I'm sorry. I just want you to think about it. Okay?"

Leaving her task, her mother sat in the chair next to her and took her by the hands. "Sweetie. You know I love you more than anything. I'm *not* giving up. But using that key would end your suffering, and give you the chance at the full life you could never get here."

Just in case it was possible for Elianna to feel any worse, her mother made it happen. She never did it on purpose, but it didn't change the pressure her mother's words put on her already slouching shoulders.

"Elizabeth," her father cut in, frustration clear in his voice. "Let it drop. She has enough on her mind."

"Alright. Alright." Her mother squeezed her hands one more time before returning to the kitchen counter to grab the plates.

"It's okay, Dad. I know I need to make a decision. It's just not easy when I don't have all the facts."

Pulling his glasses off and rubbing his eyes with his hands, her father looked exhausted. "You don't have to make one right now, Firefly. The key will still be there for you later. Let's focus on getting you better for now."

She nodded, but she knew her father was only trying to pacify her. The key may have still been there for the moment, but she didn't have much longer, and she knew it. The coughing and shortness of breath were getting worse, as was the feeling of hopelessness. If she did have many more years ahead of her, she didn't know if she could handle spending them as sick as she was.

Forcing down her dinner, knowing the medication would make it come up later, Elianna settled back into her role as the sick daughter, rolling with the punches so she wouldn't make her parents worry more than they already did. She may have been the one living with cancer, but they were all helpless.

The key taunted Elianna as she laid in her bed that night. The intricate skeleton key was an antique gold, enchanted with the magic of the fae and issued to her on the day her doctor confirmed the spread of her cancer into her lungs. She had laid the key there that night, right next to her television, and hadn't touched it since.

The more the air seemed to thin, and the more the pain in her chest grew, the more the key beckoned her like the call of a siren. All she would have to do was grab the key, go to the Shrine of Solstice, and place it in the lock. Then, if the stories were true, she would be brought into Ecromos and healed. She would never see her family again, never know if survival in the human realm had been possible, but the cancer would be gone.

Maybe, if the best of the rumors were true, she'd have a soulmate there, someone to share the rest of her much longer life with. Even with a new family, the thought of living through losing her parents was too much for her to bear. It was an impossible call.

Each key was said to link one fae male and one human female, making them destined for each other. Elianna wondered if that was why it seemed to light from within sometimes, as though he was touching his key and trying to get her attention. But what if she didn't like him? Wasn't attracted to him? Worst yet, what if he was cruel to her and treated her like a prisoner, like no more than a breeding mare? Those were all questions she didn't have the answers to, but they were all answers she needed if she was going to make a decision, if she would have to decide that leaving her world was better than staying. She laid in bed for hours thinking about it, the building pressure making the tightness in her chest even worse. Even if she died in the human realm, some fates were worse than death.

A hacking cough hit Elianna as she rested. She doubled over on the bed, her breathing becoming more ragged with the force of it. She watched the key with watering eyes and it flickered, emanating the sudden flash of light she'd only ever seen a few times. It only lasted for a moment, but she knew it had been real and not just a trick her oxygen-starved mind was playing on her. Climbing from her bed, she grabbed the magical object, feeling the unmistakable power that surged through it and into her, the compulsion for her to use it palpable.

"You've been MIA for like three days, Elli. Where have you been?" Kiera Harris placed the back of her hand on Elianna's head, pretending to check her for fever as they sat in the university's coffee shop. Elianna took classes from home, although she realized it was a waste of time, but Kiera got to live on campus and experience all the things she would never get to experience. It would have been a lie to say it didn't affect her to miss out on the experiences so many other young people took for granted, but dwelling on it wouldn't change anything except her mental health.

Elianna shrugged. "My cough got worse so my mom insisted I stay in bed and eat awful canned soup while watching reruns. You know she'd prefer it if I never left the house. It wasn't my finest few days, but I did get through two filthy novels while pretending to be studying."

Kiera laughed, taking a sip of her nonfat latte. "Elizabeth's going to find your smutty book stash one of these days and set them ablaze. Just you wait."

Rolling her eyes, Elianna tossed a straw wrapper at her friend. "Like you've got room to talk. I borrowed all those books from you."

"You're so full of it." Kiera laughed again but her face turned serious only a moment later. "When do you guys head to Kinderside to see the new specialist?"

She'd been trying to avoid thinking about it. The new specialist would say the same thing as the last eight had. It wouldn't change anything, only remind her of the pincushion she'd become. "Tomorrow, I think. I don't even keep track anymore."

The night before any doctor's visit was stressful, even if she'd lost any hope for re-mission. Elianna settled into bed, pulling out one of the naughty books she kept in her side table drawer and opening it to where she'd left off. She didn't know why she bothered hiding them from her mother. Nineteen years old was technically an adult, but her parents still treated her like she was twelve, not that she minded being taken care of.

After reading for hours, and fantasizing about the sexy fictional character in her current read who was totally going on her growing list of book boyfriends, she fell asleep with the book across her stomach.

Tightness in her chest, followed by the struggle of her lungs to take in enough air pulled Elianna from sleep. Gasping, she reached for the buzzer her parents had installed next to her bed a few months before, pressing it repeatedly to wake them. Her heart hammered against her ribcage, every attack feeling like it would be her final battle. Thankfully, it only took seconds for her mother to dart into her bedroom, followed by her father.

"I'll call the ambulance," her father said as he ran out the room to grab his phone.

Her mother leaned over the bed, securing the oxygen cannula to her nose and reaching for her inhaler on the side table. Elianna sucked in the medicine, but the inhaler brought no relief. She continued to struggle, the air in the room inadequate, even with her oxygen tube. Spots colored her vision as the decision came to her without much thought. Looking to her mother with desperation in her eyes, Elianna reached her hand toward the metal object flickering next to the television. *"Get the key."*

CHAPTER 2 ELIANNA

The golden key in Elizabeth's hand was the only indication the first responders needed to know where to take her daughter. It was a scenario they knew well enough. With the sound of the siren piercing the late night silence, the ambulance raced toward the Shrine nestled within the Haunted Mountains, the exit leading to the hospital fading in the distance. Grief was replaced by numbness, filling Elianna's ailing body with every mile they drove down the darkened roadway.

Elianna's parents hovered over her, holding her hands and whispering words of encouragement, but all she felt was nothing. Nothing, aside from the pain in her chest, and the lack of oxygen in the air. She would never see them again. It wasn't a reality she could come to terms with, so she pushed it in the back of her mind and tried to pretend she was simply going to yet another hospital visit. That way, the fallout of her decision wouldn't hit her until it was too late for her to change her mind, or take it back. By the time she would let those feelings flood back in, she would be stuck inside the realm of Ecromos, where she'd be forced to either deal with it, or she would be too preoccupied to even think about it. Either scenario would be better than letting doubt fracture her shaky resolve now that she'd finally made a decision.

When the key was placed in her hand, just as the ambulance approached the Shrine, the light within it flashed faster, more frantically as power surged through it and into her palm. It was as though touching it compelled her to follow through, as though someone on the other side was begging her to go to them. She felt the pull of the portal with every fiber of her being, but the hesitation she'd been suppressing grew as well.

By the time the vehicle parked, and her stretcher was rolled out onto the roughly laid pavement, the tears came out in sobs, uncertainty lacing every ragged breath.

"I've changed my m-mind. Mom?" With the pain in Elianna's chest, the words couldn't come out fast enough. "No. Let's go b-back to the hospital."

When her mother looked at her, silver lined her eyes, but she shook her head, the gesture crushing Elianna's heart. "Sweetheart. *Please.* This is the right decision for you."

Her father faltered, pulling the stretcher to a stop. "Maybe we should wait, Elizabeth. Clearly this isn't what she wants. She shouldn't be making this decision when she's in distress."

Another round of violent coughing hit Elianna, her body betraying her when she needed it to cooperate the most. She needed her parents to have faith that she could recover, and bring her to the hospital instead. She needed more time.

Wiping her eyes and setting her jaw with renewed determination, her mother yanked on the stretcher, forcing it to roll toward the Shrine again. "We have to do this now, Peter. If we wait," Her mother hesitated, sobbing, making her voice shake. "If we wait, it may be too late. You know the rules. They won't take her if she's too far gone. Even now, what if she's too sick? We have to do this now."

Elianna didn't argue out loud, her body in too much turmoil for her words to hold any water. She knew her mother was right, even if she didn't want to admit it, even if she wasn't ready to leave them. The truth was, she would never be ready.

"What's it gonna be, Elianna?" one of the first responders asked as he locked the stretcher in place.

It was her mother who answered. "She has to go. We have to do this now, while she still can." Elizabeth leaned over her daughter, cradling her cheeks between her hands. "Sweetheart. Your dad and I would do anything for you, and this is something we have to do. We love you too much to let you sacrifice your life for more time with us." Elianna shook her head, tears streaming from her eyes as she glanced from her mother to her father, committing their faces to memory. "After all the years you've suffered, this is your chance to be free from the pain. This is your chance to be happy."

Her father moved closer, taking her by the hand. "Your mother's right, Firefly. It's time."

Even though her mind knew her parents were right, her heart couldn't accept what they were saying, but she nodded, or something that could've been mistaken as a nod.

The Shrine of the Solstice loomed before her, a white structure that was such a contrast to the dark mountains surrounding it. The stretcher began rolling toward the entrance again, which was infinitely left open, and up the ramp that made it easier to bring in people like her. People who couldn't walk in by themselves. *Dying people.* The white marble of the building gleamed in the firelight of the candles, making the entire interior glow with a magical aura.

Although Elianna had read all about the Shrine, and had been schooled in the process of getting to the door, she'd never been inside. She'd never even been in the parking lot. The walls were covered with mosaics of the setting sun, landscapes, and plantlife, all glittering with the candle light, all seeming to be alive.

The door, a cerulean blue, stood against the back wall, framed by large sconces, the flames bigger than the rest, as though they were enchanted. They probably were. She watched the door, watched the antique lock, waiting for it to do something. *Anything.* Hoping it would give her some indication as to what she should do, what her fate would be on the other side, but it didn't. It just stood there.

Elianna's eyes darted from her parents to the first responders, the feeling of desperation growing in her once again. "Mom? I don't want to do this." Reaching for her mother's hand that gripped the railing, she pulled it to her. "Please, Mom."

The two men who brought her there looked more than uncomfortable as they watched Elianna and her parents, waiting for someone to make a decision. They didn't speak. Instead, they just watched over her oxygen and vital signs, waiting patiently for what would come next.

Elizabeth squeezed the key within her daughter's hand, before leaning over to hug her, but her eyes were distant. "I'm not saying goodbye, Sweetheart. But I know this is the right thing for you to do, and you know it too." Elianna's body shook with the force of her sobs, but she didn't bother arguing. She was in too much distress to make the right decision for herself anymore.

When her father leaned over her and wrapped his arms around her, her crying only got worse. "You're gonna shine in Ecromos, Firefly. Just wait and see."

She knew her father believed what he'd said, but she wasn't so sure. She wasn't sure about anything. Still, Elianna glanced her tear-stained eyes up at the first responders and nodded, feeling less confidence than she tried to force onto her face. Her parents held her hands as the oxygen was removed, her lungs straining without it, but she didn't object.

"You need to turn the key, Sweetheart," her mother said, releasing her hand and nudging it toward the door as the back of her stretcher was raised into the sitting position.

Without her cannula, the growing panic inside Elianna only made her breathing more erratic. She'd never felt so powerless, even when she'd received her diagnosis, even as that diagnosis had gotten worse. Her father reached behind her back, helping to lift her from the bed as the first responders supported her on weak legs. She lifted the golden key to the antique lock, her hand trembling as it aimed for the door.

Violent coughing hit her again, her chest squeezing without the extra oxygen. She doubled over as they held onto her, the key falling as though in slow motion, clanging loudly as it hit the floor.

The next moments were a blur, her oxygen starved brain processing too slow for them to make sense. She coughed against her father's chest as he cradled her on the ground, as her mother reached for the key. The scene around her spun, but only a moment seemed to pass between when she had dropped to the floor, and when her mother slammed the key into the lock and the door creaked open.

The room beyond the doorway was a white void. There was no way to see what was hiding behind the light, although Elianna wasn't sure if the brightness was from the state of her body, or if it was truly what she would be traveling into.

Placing the key back into Elianna's hand, Elizabeth kissed her daughter on the forehead, giving her one more warm smile, before moving aside. Elianna stared into the void as her father and the first responders lifted her, setting her down just within the opening. The last thing she saw before the door closed, separating her from her parents, from her world, was the silver behind her father's eyes, her mother's strength shattering.

As soon as the lock clicked into place, Elianna collapsed, the light enveloping her.

Elianna wasn't sure how much time had passed since she'd been left on the inside of the doorway, inside the endless sea of white, nor was she sure if she was still alive. Snippets of visions flashed in and out of her consciousness. The feeling of hands touching her, images of people surrounding her. *Voices.* She couldn't focus on one thing. She was too weak, too exhausted. The coughing had subsided, her breathing becoming easier, but she didn't have the strength to analyze why. Maybe she was dead. A brief moment of panic was all she felt before oblivion consumed her once again.

The room Elianna woke in was stark, empty aside from a small bed, table, sink, and toilet. The walls were a sterile white, as were the sheets, and even the gown she was wearing. It was so void of color, that it made her wonder if she was still in the spot she'd been left in when her parents had closed her into the portal. There were no windows, and no handle on the door. She was trapped, imprisoned, but too confused to panic just yet.

Chest no longer hurting, Elianna was able to take the first deep breath she'd been allowed in more than four years. Maybe she *was* dead. A whimpering sob rose in her throat but she held it down as sounds echoed on the other side of the door. Crouching in the corner, she waited for the door to open, waited for some indication of whether she was in the other world, or if her time of being alive had ended.

"Oh, good. You're awake." An older woman walked into the room with a tray balanced in her hands. No. Not a woman. *Fae.* She had to be.

Iridescent wings, similar to that of a dragonfly, were tucked against her back as she turned to set a food tray on the small table near the wall. Her skin was tinged with lilac, her ears slightly pointed. Her face, aside from the color of her skin and the obsidian of her eyes, looked almost human. Even her hair, a thick black braid, fell down the center of her back like women of the human world. It made Elianna all the more self conscious about her own hair, or lack thereof, which had only just begun growing back since her chemotherapy, and barely tucked behind her ears in a chestnut pixie cut. Smoothing her hands against it, she watched her visitor.

Although the female's sweet voice, and equally sugary smile, was disarming, Elianna's heart still thrummed too quickly in her chest. She'd never needed her mother as badly as she did at that moment. "Where am I?"

Freezing for only a moment as she readied a cup of tea, the female seemed to be caught off guard at Elianna's question. When she turned back around with the steaming mug in her hands, the saccharine smile was still on her face. "Well, you're at Lord Argall's manor in the Court of Knowledge, Miss. And my name is Hiedra. I'll be tending to you while you're here. What's your name?"

The statement made her stomach clench, the implications of it reminding her of the fears she'd harbored before using the key. "My name is Elianna…" She hesitated, scanning the room. "I thought the key would be bringing me to my mate, the one with the twin to my key. Where will I be going once I leave here?"

She looked around the room for her golden key, but didn't see it anywhere. *They'd taken it.* An ominous feeling crawled over her, seeping into any part of her that had previously held any hope.

Hiedra shrugged and reached for the bowl of soup. "I don't know anything about a mate, Miss. You came to us rather sick and it took a lot to heal you. But, as I understand it, you'll be with a new master as soon as you're all fixed up."

A master. The words hit Elianna like a bullet to the chest, her worst fears coming to life. She was a prisoner.

Grab The Other World to continue reading!

Blaze's point of view is next!

https://a.co/d/efCuSjD

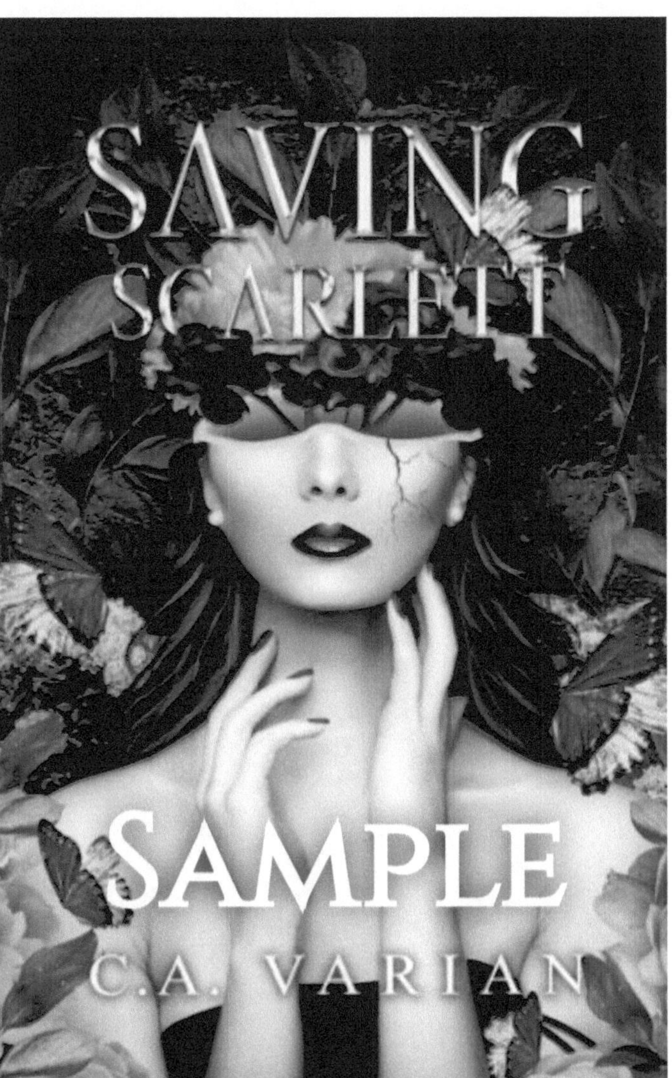

SAVING
SCARLETT
SAMPLE
C.A. VARIAN

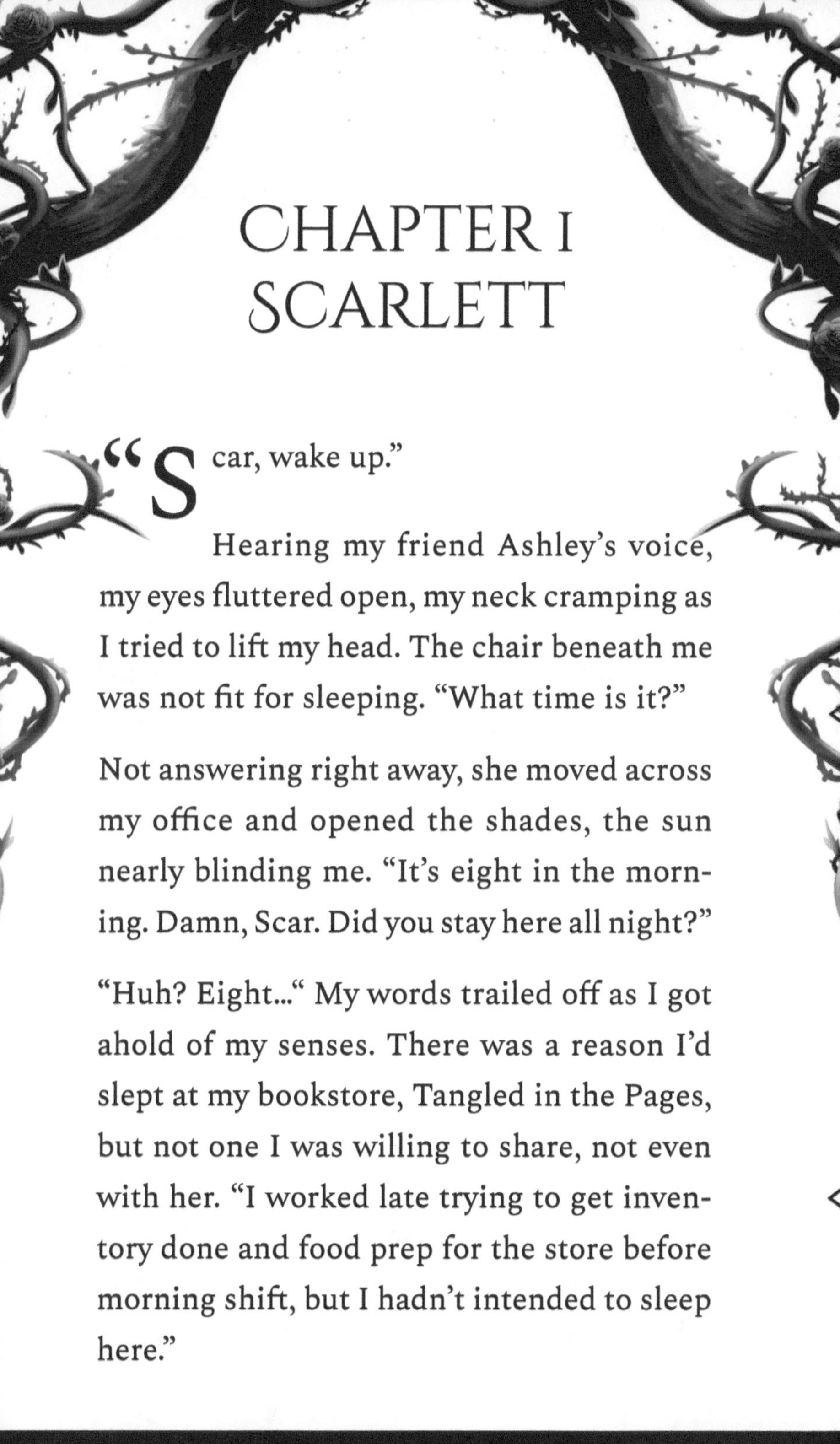

CHAPTER 1
SCARLETT

"Scar, wake up."

Hearing my friend Ashley's voice, my eyes fluttered open, my neck cramping as I tried to lift my head. The chair beneath me was not fit for sleeping. "What time is it?"

Not answering right away, she moved across my office and opened the shades, the sun nearly blinding me. "It's eight in the morning. Damn, Scar. Did you stay here all night?"

"Huh? Eight..." My words trailed off as I got ahold of my senses. There was a reason I'd slept at my bookstore, Tangled in the Pages, but not one I was willing to share, not even with her. "I worked late trying to get inventory done and food prep for the store before morning shift, but I hadn't intended to sleep here."

Shaking her head, Ashley placed a cup of coffee in my hand. "Do you want to go home and change? Maybe put some ice on that. How in the hell did you do that to yourself?"

When she pointed at my face, I lost all ability to breathe, my lungs seizing as images of what had happened the day before flooded into my head—the beating he'd given me—again. I lifted my fingers to my cheek, touching the area where my eye was swollen. Grinning, I feigned embarrassment. No one knew my shameful secret. "Oh. Yeah. I took a book to the eye last night. I must not have pushed it all the way onto the shelf."

Ashley turned a side eye in my direction. "You know I'll help you with inventory. All you have to do is ask. Especially since you seem to keep getting more and more clumsy these days. How old are you again? Eighty?"

Huffing a laugh, I took a deep sip of the coffee, closing my eyes as it fed my caffeine addiction. "I'm thirty and I was just tired. That's what I get for working so late every night, but I can't seem to help myself. This place is my dream, after all."

While I dug in my purse for headache medication, she left my office and began working on the opening procedures.

Once Ashley put the money into the register, she returned to me, looking more closely at my injury. I hissed as she touched it, even though her hand was gentle.

"You may need to have that looked at in case you have a concussion. And go home at night, Scar. Work can wait until the next morning."

I grinned and nodded. There was so much I wanted to tell my friend but couldn't, or at least, *wouldn't*. "I'll go home and take a shower. Are you sure you'll be okay while I'm gone? Can I bring you back something to eat?"

With a shake of her head, she all but shoved me toward the door. "We have pastries here.

I'll be fine. Now go and get yourself presentable and put on lots of concealer."

When I got in my car, I checked my phone and was relieved to have no messages. My husband, Joshua, knew I was at the store and had not called to check up on me. I wasn't surprised. He'd probably gone straight to his mistress the moment I'd left the house. All I hoped was that he wasn't home when I got there.

Sucking in a breath as my reality threatened to pour fresh tears out of my bruised eye, I turned up the radio, hoping the music could drown out the thoughts running through my head, all of them telling me to run away.

Since no one was home when I arrived at my house, I took a quick shower and packed an overnight bag, just in case I fell asleep in my bookstore again. It didn't have a bed, but it was still a safe place where I could hide out when I needed to.

By the time I made it back to Tangled in the Pages, my bookstore and coffee shop combo was in full swing. Ashley was taking orders while another employee, Jack, was preparing the food and drinks. Ashley looked up at me as the bell jingled over the door, her eyes telling me they were swamped and needed help. It was the exact reason I had been hesitant to leave in the first place.

Tossing my bags in my office and locking the door, I returned to the front of the store and took over register duty so Ashley could help Jack. With the holidays coming, it was our busiest time of year, which made me wonder if I needed to hire a few more employees to help during the rushes. I'd only had the store for a few years, so it was still a new adventure for me.

I moved to the counter, pouring fresh coffee and greeting customers with practiced ease. The familiar routine calmed my frayed nerves, allowing me to push aside the lingering fear and anxiety. I was safe there in my space, surrounded by the things and people I loved.

"The usual?" I asked an older gentleman, Henry, who came in every morning. He nodded, eyes crinkling behind wire-rimmed glasses.

"You're a lifesaver, Scarlett." His voice was warm, full of affection. "Don't know what I'd do without my morning coffee and chat."

"You'd find another coffee shop," I teased, sliding his coffee across the counter and waving away his attempt to pay. "On the house today, Henry. You deserve it."

"Well, aren't you a sweetheart." Smile deepening, he patted my hand before moving to the chair by the window and burying himself in the newspaper I always set aside for him.

Bumping my shoulder, Ashley nodded at the few customers waiting to be served. "You okay?"

"Yeah." I drew in a steadying breath, meeting her concerned gaze. "I'm okay. Just tired."

"I'm here if you need anything." Her brown eyes were warm, full of affection. She'd been with me since the beginning. "Always."

"I know." I smiled, small but genuinely. "Thank you. For everything."

Smiling, she nudged me again. "Anytime. Now come on, time to get back to work!"

I laughed, following her lead as we set about serving the new customers who'd lined up at the register. With the warmth of an environment I created myself, the familiar routine eased the lingering ache in my chest.

Once the morning rush had calmed, I wiped the dust from the shelves and straightened the stacks of books, admiring my cozy bookstore. The aroma of fresh coffee wafted through the air, mingling with the soft jazz music playing over the speakers. Even if I hadn't owned the store, I realized I would probably spend all my time there. It was the exact way I wanted my customers to feel.

My muscles ached from unloading inventory for hours the night before, but a familiar peace settled over me. My bookstore was my sanctuary, a refuge from a world that had been cruel and unforgiving for too long.

As I bustled around the space, a young couple lounged on the sofa near the fireplace, sipping lattes and reading from well-worn paperbacks. The fireplace didn't get much use, since it was hot as Hades in Louisiana most of the year, but it was still a beautiful feature of the building. Two teenage girls giggled over their cinnamon rolls at a table near the front window and an older man tapped away on his laptop in the corner, a half-empty mug of Earl Grey tea beside him. *My regulars.* They came for the atmosphere as much as for the books and coffee.

Leaning against the counter, I breathed in the familiar scents, feeling tension ease from my shoulders. My gaze wandered to the worn wooden floors and shelves lining the walls, filled with stories of adventure, heartbreak and hope. There were so many lives and worlds contained within the pages to get lost in. I only wished I had more time to read.

A smile tugged at my lips as another wave of customers trickled through the door. My perfect, imperfect world. The one I had built from nothing.

This was my story.

My happily ever after.

Joshua couldn't take that away from me.

Noticing that a group of college kids had left a stack of books on a small table near the back of the store, which was a daily occurrence, I scooped them up, intending to put

them away. I had just started returning them to the shelves when the bell above the door chimed, drawing my gaze. A man stepped inside, tall and broad-shouldered, clad in black from head to toe. Jet black hair fell over piercing blue eyes as he paused just inside the entrance, scanning the room. His gaze was sharp, intense, taking in everything and missing nothing.

Unease flickered through me at his imposing presence, at odds with the cozy atmosphere of my shop. And yet...curiosity stirred as I studied him from beneath my lashes. There was a hardness to his expression, as if he had seen and endured far too much in his life, although he couldn't have been much older than me. But something about his lingering gaze and the way one corner of his mouth tilted upward tugged at my interest and I had to admit, he was sexy as hell.

A mystery waiting to be solved.

His gaze landed on a shelf of tattered paperbacks along the far wall and the hint of a smile softened his angular features. My heart skipped as he strode forward, boots thudding against the wooden floor, and slid out a worn copy of *Treasure Island*.

Interest sparked in those fathomless light blue eyes as he flipped through the pages, as if transported to another time and place. A place of adventure and danger and...*longing*.

Heat crept into my cheeks. I was reading too much into a simple glance and smile, letting my imagination run wild. The stranger was just a customer, here to browse the shelves like any other.

Surprising even myself, I moved across the room, my hands smoothing the front of my apron as I stepped forward to greet him.

I cleared my throat, my pulse quickening like I was an unpopular school girl asking the popular guy to prom. "Find anything interesting?"

Glancing up from the book, a flicker of surprise crossed his expression, as if he hadn't expected me to approach. Still, his lips curved into a slow, devastating smile that did dangerous things to my heart.

"A childhood favorite." As though fate only meant to be crueler, his voice was as smooth and dark as aged whiskey. He held up the book. "Treasure Island ignited my love for adventure at a young age."

"Mine as well." I leaned a hip against the shelf, hoping I appeared more at ease than I felt. Inside, my body was buzzing. "The pirates, the danger, the thrill of discovering treasure. Stevenson was a master storyteller."

"That he was." Sliding the book back into place, he turned to face me fully, arms loosely crossing over his chest. Even with my heels, I had to tilt my head back to meet his gaze. "You have an interesting collection here. Not what one would expect in a small coffee shop."

"I'm glad you think so." Although I shrugged, a flush of pride rushed through me. "Books have always been my passion. There's nothing quite like getting lost in a good story, discovering new worlds and characters."

"An escape from reality." His tone had gone pensive, as if he understood that need on a deeper level. "And a glimpse into the lives of others, to remind us we're not alone."

I stared at him, struck by the insight. He saw it, the power of stories—of words—to transcend our circumstances and forge connections.

A slow smile curved my lips. "It seems we have more in common than a love for *Treasure Island*, Mr...?"

He blinked, as if realizing he hadn't introduced himself. "Bane."

Our gazes held for a long moment, a strange tension simmering between us. I couldn't look away from his eyes, pale blue and piercing, and I realized at that moment that his name was an omen. Something told me this man could destroy me and I would love every second of it.

Reminding myself that I was indeed married and that I shouldn't think such things, I licked my dry lips, all too aware of my heartbeat quickening. "Bane," I repeated. Even as I was berating myself for the awkward response, one corner of his mouth lifted in a half-smile that nearly threw my equilibrium off balance. "It's a pleasure."

"The pleasure is mine…?" He posed it as a question, obviously waiting for my name.

"I'm Scarlett."

Bane's gaze dipped to my mouth and then lower, a slow perusal that had heat pooling low in my belly. I shifted on my feet, torn between embarrassment at my reaction and a reckless urge to move closer to him, to close the space between us.

When his eyes returned to mine, a knowing glint lit their depths. As if he sensed the effect he had on me. As if he relished it. I didn't doubt he had that effect on all the ladies.

A blush stained my cheeks and I took a step back, breaking the spell. "Well," I said, a bit breathless, "let me know if you need any more book recommendations. I'm always here."

"I'll be sure to do that." Amusement lurked in his tone and he gave a slight bow of his head. "It was a pleasure meeting you, Scarlett."

Saving me from embarrassing myself any further, the bell above the door jingled, telling me new customers had entered the store. I smiled at him once more before turning to look back toward the counter, my hands twisting in my apron.

"That's my cue, but if you come to the register, I would be happy to give you a cup of coffee—on the house, of course. Since you have such good taste in books."

CHAPTER 2 BANE

The moonlight glinted off the blade of my favorite knife as I crept through the shadows toward my target. My footsteps were silent, my breathing steady. I was in my element.

Pausing behind a pillar, my eyes scanned the lavish ballroom before they fell on Auguste LaRoche, the corrupt businessman who had made far too many enemies. His receding hairline did nothing to hide the look of smug entitlement on his face as he laughed loudly with a group of partygoers. Little did he know those would be the last laughs he ever shared. Moving away from the group, he lifted his whiskey to his mouth, watching his guests.

I adjusted my grip on the knife, the leather of my gloves creaking ever so slightly. LaRoche's personal bodyguards stood several feet away, oblivious to the predator in their midst. *Fools.* Their complacency would cost their boss his life.

In one swift movement, I slipped behind LaRoche and pressed the cold steel to his throat, pulling him behind the pillar with me. His laughter transformed into a strangled gasp. The bodyguards whirled around, hands flying to their hip holsters, but they were too late. I'd already pulled him into a back hallway—out of sight.

"Please, I'll give you anything. Just don't—"

His begging turned into a gurgle as I slashed the knife across his throat, scarlet spilling down his white tuxedo shirt as he collapsed onto the white marble floor. As chaos erupted in the ballroom a moment later when his guards undoubtedly found him, I was already gone, disappearing into the night.

Another contract was completed. It was another day my niece would live to see, thanks to the funds from the night's kill. For her, I would paint the world red. For her, I would be a monster.

The sterile scent of antiseptic hit my nose as I walked through the automatic doors of the hospital. So late at night, the lights in the hallways were dimmed, the bustling crowds of the daytime replaced by the soft footsteps of nurses on night shift. I made my way to the pediatric intensive care unit, the one place in this world that made my chest constrict with emotion. It was past visiting hours, but no one ever stopped me from entering when I showed up. My money paid for part of their salary.

I nodded to the nurse at the desk before continuing to room four hundred and twenty eight—Evelyn's room. Pushing the door open with a gentle hand, my eyes landed on my seven-year-old niece's tiny body laying motionless in the bed, the steady beep of the heart monitor the only indication she still clung to life. Her skin was pale, her bald head covered by a pink knitted cap. Dark circles stood out under her closed eyes, eyes that should have been filled with joy and laughter rather than pain.

Pulling a chair up next to her bed, I took her tiny hand in mine. So delicate, so fragile. Hard to believe that little hand once felt strong enough to grab onto my fingers as I swung her around the yard.

"Hey kiddo," I whispered. "I'm back."

No response, not that I expected one. The experimental treatment kept her unconscious most days, her body too weak to face the world. But I knew on some level she could sense I was there.

"I did it. I got the money for your next treatment." My voice caught, wishing I could take away her pain. "So you just hang in there. You're going to get better soon, I promise."

Bringing her hand up to my lips, I kissed it before setting it back down. I had to believe she would recover. The alternative was too agonizing to face.

"I love you, Evie. Be strong for me."

I sat with her a while longer, keeping a silent vigil over her fragile form. For her, I would walk through the fires of hell. For her, I would make sure she survived—no matter the cost.

The door opened and I turned to see my sister entering, her black hair pulled back into a messy bun. Dark circles stood out under her eyes as well, testament to the many sleepless nights she'd spent at Evelyn's bedside.

Sitting beside me, Caroline placed a delicate hand on my shoulder. "She's fighting hard. Our girl's a warrior."

I nodded, a lump forming in my throat. Evelyn was the strongest person I knew, enduring endless treatments and pain with seldom a complaint.

Tapping the white, two-by-three piece of cardstock in my hand, I listened as the stiff-shirt CEO across from me droned on about the hit he wanted to take out on his unsuspecting wife and exactly how he wanted it done. Killing was my thing. It was the one thing I was really fucking good at, and I didn't need this asshole telling me how to do my job. Still, I didn't interrupt him. The more he spoke, the redder his face became, and I secretly hoped he would have a heart attack and keel over in his chair. I already had his payment in my pocket, a stack of unmarked bills that he wasn't getting back, even if he did croak in front of me.

Whenever I met with a potential client for the first time, I always tried to come up with their story in my head first just to see how close I was—just to see how good I was at reading people. This guy was easy, no matter how hard he tried to convince me otherwise. He wanted to convince me that his wife was evil incarnate, the devil in disguise, but it all came down to greed. That's all it ever was for these white-collar assholes looking for a hit on their spouses.

From what I gathered, he wanted her out of the way but he wanted to keep all the money. Simply put, his mistress was pregnant, and he wanted to marry her. Out with the old and in with the new. He knew if his wife found out, she would take him for all he was worth, but if she died... If his wife died in any way other than suicide, he would make a killing on her life insurance. *Pun intended.* Then, he would be able to marry his current mistress and find a new side piece as well. In other words, he would be able to move on with his life by repeating the cycle.

I could make it look like an accident or even a home robbery, and I wasn't there to question *why* he wanted her dead. There was no reason for him to tell me half of the shit that came tumbling out of his mouth. In my line of work, I tried to stay away from all that. I didn't care why someone ordered a hit or whether the target was a modern-day saint. My job was simple: take out the target and make money. Period. Whether his wife was the devil or the sweetest woman on the planet, I didn't give a shit. What he really needed was a therapist to talk to, even his barber would do, someone he could ramble to for a few hours to make him feel important. I had better things to do.

The underground club we sat in was a shady place in downtown New Orleans, but I'd chosen it specifically because I knew no one inside would speak a word of our meeting. Even though I didn't own the club, and the owner didn't even know my real name, he was indebted to me for a big job I'd done for him in the past. As far as the other patrons, most of them were so strung out that they wouldn't even remember being there themselves by the time they woke up in the morning, if they woke up at all.

As the clock ticked, I looked at my phone, pretending to get a message so he would get the hint that he needed to stop talking. "All I need to know is a general timeline and where to find her. I have to go, so if that's all…"

I pushed back in my chair, standing to leave, when he slid a slip of paper across the table. "This is my address. I'll be out of town next week at a business conference. She should be home alone then."

Thinking he was done speaking, *finally*, I turned to walk away when he grabbed my wrist.

I came very close to knocking him unconscious for touching me, but I clenched my jaw and turned back to look at him. "Don't ever put your hands on me," I growled, pulling out of his grip. "Not if you want to keep them."

Knowing what was good for him, he backed away, holding his hands up in supplication. "I'm sorry. I'm sorry. I just wanted to add the code to our security system so you can get inside the house."

Annoyance still boiling in my blood, I handed the paper back to him, scanning the club again as he scribbled some digits onto it. We'd been in there for way too long. I never let my meetings go on for that long, and I should have shut him down twenty minutes earlier, but I was amusing myself with how talking about his wife turned his face the color of a firetruck.

The moment he held the paper back out to me, I yanked it out of his hand, and walked away. Slipping the paper into my pocket, I walked out of the bar and back into the alley.

As I strolled toward my downtown apartment, I couldn't help but chuckle. How big of an idiot was he to give the security code to get into his home to a known killer? It was then that I decided that I would definitely pay them a visit—*before* he left for his trip. Since I had the keys to the castle, I may as well have a little bit of fun.

Enjoying Saving Scarlett? The eBook releases in January and you can grab it here:

https://www.amazon.com/dp/B0CJR92XW2

But you can grab the signed paperback and hardback early through my TikTok shop! There's even a special edition!

C.A. VARIAN

Song of Death

SUPERNATURAL SAVIOR'S SERIES
BOOK ONE

Sample

CHAPTER 1
AZURE

"Help!" Azure Galanides screamed as the current pulled her little sister under the tumultuous waves. "Someone! Please! Save her!"

She had only taken her eyes off the seven-year-old for a moment, but that was enough for Daneliya to drift out of her reach. No one was on the beach. They were on their own.

Running into the rough waters, Azure tried to grasp her sister's hand, but the child only thrashed, before going under the surface once more, pulled further into the current. Sobs poured freely out of Azure, salty tears mixing with the brine of the Lamalis Sea.

"Someone! Please!"

Daneliya did not surface again. Panicked, Azure jumped forward and sucked in a deep breath as she dove under. She searched for a sign of the child, but opening her eyes was useless. The dark waters burned, obscuring her vision. She couldn't see anything.

She flailed her limbs violently, feeling around for her sister in the rough seas, but her hands found nothing. Her lungs protested, forcing her up for air, but a wave crashed over her and almost forced her under once more. She choked and sputtered as the water assaulted her nose and mouth before she could inhale.

Tiny arms drifted toward her with the next crest. Reaching out, she grabbed her sister as she fought the push and pull of the current in a desperate attempt to reach the beach. Storm clouds hovered ominously above, completely blocking out the sun, as she laid her sister's limp body on the sandy shore. The eerie darkness that swallowed up the calm afternoon gave the deserted coast a sinister feeling.

"Daneliya!" Azure sobbed as she shook her sister's body. The adolescent had turned a sickening shade of blue, but she couldn't give up. "Please! Someone! Help us!" She pushed on the child's chest frantically, desperate to expel the water from her little lungs, but it was useless. There was no sign of the color receding, no sign of breath.

A flash of lightning cracked across the darkening sky as Azure wept over her sister's tiny frame. Daneliya was gone. She'd lost her, and it was all her fault. The seven-year-old was her responsibility, and she failed to keep her safe.

At eighteen years old, Azure knew better than to take her eyes off the child for even a moment. With that one mistake, she had killed the last of her family—the only person she had left in this life. She'd already lost her parents, and now Daneliya, too. There was no one left and no more reason for her to carry on.

Looking over her shoulder at the violent waves that took her sister from her, Azure considered meeting the same end. All she had to do was walk in and let go. There was no point in persevering anymore. The air thickened around her, feeling heavy against her skin, as she looked down at Daneliya's lifeless body once more. Once the waves took her, the pain of being the only survivor would disappear. Everything would disappear. The agony that small mistake caused, the feeling of her heart wrenching in two, would end.

The humidity continued to condense until water droplets formed and hung around her, suspended in midair. An icy hand touched her shoulder, jolting her to the side. Azure whipped her head around, but no one was there. Although it was midday, the sky had darkened so much that it looked like night. She shook off her grim thoughts and bent to lift her sister's body, intending to remove her from the beach and bring her somewhere safe, but the invisible hand touched her shoulder again. Freezing in place, Azure sucked in a deep breath before looking up.

Her eyes darted to the side, spotting a hooded figure beside her, its face hidden in shadows. Although she couldn't explain it, power seemed to radiate out from them, encircling her and holding her in place. She couldn't make out the face of the being as it loomed over her like a silent sentinel—an overseeing god with no empathy for its people. *Watching, but not helping.*

"Help her. Please." Azure wept over her sister, defeated and shivering, as her voice came out as a whispered plea. She knew Daneliya was beyond saving, but she still begged for a miracle.

The cloaked individual lowered themselves over the young girl's body, placing a pale hand on the child's still chest. It did not rise and fall. There were no signs of life. She was gone. Azure's breath caught in her throat as she continued to plead.

"Can you help her? Please. I'll do anything."

Silence filled the shoreline in the place of her sister's beating heart. It was enough to make Azure wonder if the being was a figment of her imagination.

"Would you trade yourself?" The hooded figure didn't look at Azure as it spoke, but the voice was feminine. Azure swallowed back the bitter dread the words invoked within her. She understood the question, but still hoped she had misunderstood, almost afraid to answer.

"Trade myself how?"

"Her soul for yours." The voice was icy and devoid of emotion, sending shivers across Azure's body, chilling her blood.

"Yes." Azure's response was only a whisper, but there was no question. *Yes.* She would trade her life for her sister's. Daneliya was too young to die.

Freezing fingers grasped Azure's hand without warning. The figure's grip was crushing as its jagged nails tore into her flesh.

"Stop! You're hurting me!" She whimpered as she struggled to pull her hand away, but it was no use. The hold only tightened further. There was no response as she watched droplets of her crimson blood soak into the golden sand. When the hooded woman let go and returned her hand to Daneliya's chest, Azure cradled her bleeding appendage. She was unsure of what to say or do as she watched her sister's body, silently praying for life to return to her bluish complexion while the mysterious woman muttered unintelligible words to herself.

Time stood still. The only sounds were Azure's thundering heart and the shallow whispers of her breath. She squeezed her eyes closed and forced herself to take a deep breath, exhaling slowly to steady herself, as she silently begged the universe to bring her sister back.

After a few painfully uneventful moments, a forceful gasp escaped Daneliya's mouth, followed by a frantic attempt to suck in air. The world spun around Azure at the miraculous sight, making it difficult to breathe.

"Return to these waters before the sun descends. If you do not, you will not live to see the morning."

The words were cold, distant. Azure turned to face the dark figure with skeptical questions on her tongue, but before she could speak, the figure disappeared. She wanted to ask who the woman was, wanted to thank her, but there was no trace of her having ever been there, except for the fact that Daneliya was alive.

The sun peeked from behind the clouds, warming her skin with its brilliant rays, as her sister's eyes opened.

"Sissy?" Daneliya's tiny voice was strained and unsure. Crushing the girl against her chest, Azure clung to her little sister as though she were afraid the child would disappear just as her savior had. Tears of joy mingled with the salty water that soaked the little girl's dress. Lifting the shivering child in her arms, Azure headed back toward their home just as the birds began to sing.

"It's okay. Everything will be okay."

CHAPTER 2 AZURE

3 YEARS LATER

Azure hissed through her clenched teeth as the burning, torn skin of her back throbbed.

"Hold still. I'm almost done." Ocevia blew on her back as she screwed the lid back on the ointment tin. "They should scab over soon. If you would stop defying her, she would stop having you whipped."

Although she knew Ocevia was right, Azure still rolled her eyes. It was no secret that she couldn't seem to stay out of trouble. Ever since she gave up her life to save her sister's, and was forced into servitude under the sea, she had been in nonstop trouble. The Sea Goddess, Miris, was difficult to please.

"Even if I stayed out of trouble, she would still find a reason to punish me."

"You're probably right." Her friend rinsed her hands in the salty water. Waves crashed violently against their small cove, making it a dangerous place to rest. At least for humans. Mermaids like them, however, spent many daylight hours on the small, rocky islands that dotted the Lamalis Sea. "Are you going to be ready to go back out tonight?"

Azure glanced at the markings she had carved in the rock wall at the back of the cave. One hundred and forty-three carvings stared back at her, and the five thousand she needed never felt so unattainable. She needed to collect five thousand souls to pay her debt to Miris. Then, if the Sea Goddess was to be believed, Azure would be free to return to her human life... if Daneliya even remembered her. She let out a shuddering breath as she gazed back at her friend. "I don't think I have a choice. My back can't take any more lashings just yet."

Ocevia pursed her lips, brushing her long blond hair away from her beautiful, delicate face. She and Azure were the same age, although the blond mermaid looked so much younger.

All the mermaids were stunning. It helped them claim their targets. Their angelic voices and beautiful features made it easy to lure men to their deaths. The humans wrecked their ships in the rough seas and drowned within the waves for a chance to claim a mermaid as their own. Every soul they claimed fed the beasts that were Miris and her henchmen, who held the chains of the mermaids and enforced their life debts.

"You really don't. You'll never be free if you keep putting more marks on your back than on that wall." Ocevia gestured to the back of the cave as she held Azure's stare.

Azure sat up with a grunt, wincing as the wounds on her back stretched with the movement. Her friend was right. She didn't know how many lashes she had taken the day before, since she'd passed out after the first few, but she had definitely taken more lashes than souls over the past three years.

"Yea... that's going to hurt you for a while." The blond mermaid grimaced as Azure moved in slow, careful motions to avoid aggravating the fresh wounds.

"I'm aware. I'm the one who always takes the whip, after all. Have you ever even been punished by Miris?"

Ocevia looked out over the horizon, her gaze vacant as she inhaled. The smell of briny water filled the moist air of the cave, as the sound of waves crashing against the jagged rocks echoed throughout the enclosed space. She remained silent for a long time before she answered Azure's question. "I have not." Ocevia shook her head, the cloudy look in her eye clearing as she continued. "It's a stormy one today. Bad for the sailors, good for us."

Sighing, Azure pulled her top back over her breasts. It was not much more than a strip of seaweed, but there was no place for modesty in her life—not anymore. Everything about her was meant to allure her victims now. "I don't consider it good for me either. I never wanted to be a killer."

Their stares locked, and Ocevia's brilliant turquoise eyes softened at Azure's words. "The water takes lives. We're just bystanders."

Azure let out an incredulous huff as she tucked her onyx hair behind her ear. The wavy locks still felt foreign to her, having taken on a violet sheen in her transformation. Nothing remained the same after becoming a mermaid. As she stared at a puddle that pooled on the cave floor, her reflection taunted her. Turquoise eyes, the same shade as every other mermaid, stared back at her as if to remind her that she was far from the human she'd once been.

Carefully crawling to her feet, she joined her friend at the mouth of the cave. Although they could shift into a human form and use their legs, they were forbidden from entering any lands where humans dwelled. Caves and small, uninhabited islands were where they rested when they left the sea. Some chose to spend their moments of respite in underwater caverns, or in the Sea Goddess' underwater palace, but Azure preferred to stay as far from Miris as she could when given the chance. "That's just wishful thinking, and you know it. Most of those ships would make it safely across if it were not for us. She has turned us into monsters. The water is the weapon, but we are the ones who wield it to claim the victims."

Ocevia sniffed as she turned away, wiping her cheek. "We don't have a choice, Azure. You try to deny our fate, but all it does is get you whipped. It's not getting you any closer to seeing your sister again. Surely you must know this."

The thought of Daneliya growing up without her sent her heart plummeting into her stomach. Azure's voice softened as the emotions ate away at her insides. "I know." She placed her hand on her friend's icy elbow. "Look, I'm sorry. I just hate this."

Wrapping Azure in an embrace, Ocevia silently cried on her friend's shoulder. "I do too. We are all in this together. None of us want to live like this."

Azure snorted. "I can think of a few who might. *The merbitches.*" Oona and Lucia, two mermaids she despised, had fulfilled their life debts long ago but remained in this cursed form, forsaking their human lives. They enjoyed being monsters who played as though they were gods with innocent mortal lives. They were evil and vicious to their very cores.

Ocevia, her only friend, nodded against her shoulder. The blond beauty was not a monster. If anything, she was the kindest among the forsaken merfolk. She'd been paying off her life debt since she was a young girl. If she remembered her life prior to her transformation, she didn't talk about it, but it had not hardened her. She was not defiant like

Azure. She followed the rules, and her back was as unblemished as her record. Azure didn't know what her friend had received in exchange for her extensive life debt, but the fact that Ocevia owed fifty thousand souls to Miris was enough to tell her it was something *big*. Ocevia had never offered an explanation, and Azure wasn't even sure if her friend had any memory of the exchange.

"Come on. Let's get something to eat."

She changed the subject, hoping to distract from the sadness her words had invoked within her friend, as she led the way to the crates that lined the far wall. Azure grabbed a few pieces of the dried fish that made up the bulk of their meals, aside from any fresh fish they ate while in the sea.

Honestly, she was tired of fish. She had never enjoyed eating them before she entered the salty waters as a slave to the wicked, and that didn't change with her transformation. Sometimes, she got to eat fruits and vegetables on one of the small islands that speckled

the sea, but it wasn't often enough for her tastes.

Giving Ocevia a handful of the small fish, they sat on the stone platform that served as a bed.

"I could really go for something other than dried fish right now." Ocevia held her nose as she took a bite.

Azure snickered. "Me too. I don't remember my mother's cooking, but my father made a tasty stuffed goose. I could go for either at this moment."

"That sounds delicious. I don't actually re-member my mother's cooking either, but I can imagine she was great at it." Her friend's voice became softer, melancholier. "When I gain my freedom, you must take me to meet your family."

Azure's heart thudded as she thought of her family. "All that's left is my little sister. I hope she found a home with someone who cares for her. With only one hundred and forty-three souls after three years, my sister will be grown and married by the time I'm free. With my luck, she will have moved away, and I'll never be able to find her."

"I'm sorry, Azure. I didn't mean to bring that up. I didn't realize about your parents."

Azure squeezed Ocevia's hand. "No. It's okay. It's my fault for never telling you about them. I've moved past that loss."

"I understand. It's hard to bring up things that cause us pain, especially when we are supposed to be hardened out here."

Her friend could not be more correct. Hardening their hearts was the only way to survive this captivity. If she didn't, watching the life drain from the drowning victims, after witnessing her own sister suffer the same fate, would be enough to break her.

Azure met Ocevia's eyes. "And what about your family? Will I ever be able to meet them?"

No matter how much Azure tried to open the conversation, her friend never spoke about her past.

Sighing, Ocevia fidgeted with the shell necklace that never left her neck. "Maybe someday."

Ocevia's noncommittal response held no hope. Azure didn't know for sure, but something told her she would never be able to meet her friend's family.

The storm was raging by the time Azure and Ocevia dared to leave their cave. The crashing waves would aid them in sinking ships and claiming souls, but the stormy weather would also limit the number of ships traversing the sea.

Azure didn't know if she was glad for the weather or not. She needed to send souls into the sea to reduce her life debt to Miris, but taking lives weighed heavily on her conscience, and she wasn't even sure if it was worth it. The likelihood of her little sister still living in their old cottage, especially by the time Azure finished paying off her life debt, was minimal. Daneliya would be long gone by the time she ended five thousand innocent lives. Any other thought was just an unrealistic dream.

"Usual spot?" Ocevia shifted forms, her human legs replaced with an iridescent turquoise tail as she dropped to sit on the edge of the rock.

Their usual spot was near the southern shipping channel, closest to the Kingdom of Thatia, Azure's homeland. Although ships could navigate through many parts of the sea, they often stayed near the same stretches of water, because they were deeper than the areas near the coast.

Most of the ships in the channel belonged to merchants that brought goods from the mainland of Thatia to the other coastal kingdoms of Avrearyn, Zourin, and Vidaica. But there were also pirate ships that sought to do harm on those seas. Because the pirates were dangerous nuisances, the mermaids typically aimed to sink those ships first, but merchants were also fair targets.

"Our usual spot works for me."

Sitting next to her friend on the rocks, Azure shifted her legs into her iridescent purple tail and slid into the cold water, disappearing below the surface. Her stomach always sank when they headed for their spot. She constantly fought an internal battle about whether she could escape from her captivity. But she couldn't. The only way to get rid of her tail permanently was to fulfill her obligations to the Sea Goddess. It was either that, or to die. If there was another way, she didn't know of it. So, with Ocevia by her side, and her heart leaden in her stomach, the two set out to claim, albeit begrudgingly, more lives.

The storm was so violent they had to swim below the surface to avoid mouthfuls of salty water. Because of the storm, the water was frigid, although Azure had become more acclimated to the extreme temperatures during her time as a slave. It was the only thing she had gotten used to. Unlike when she was human, her skin no longer shriveled after long stints in the sea, and she was able to dry off much quicker than before. Everything was different now. Even her voice had gotten clearer, and her ability to sing was more fine-tuned. These changes made claiming lives easier, but her conscience could not be overlooked. Her aversion to the task grew with each soul she was forced to steal.

They arrived at their usual hunting grounds an hour later and lifted their heads above the surface, scanning the horizon. There were no boats around at that moment, but they waited for one to show up, anyway. The thunderstorm continued to rage, making it difficult to see very far. Lightning struck in the distance, flashing brilliantly against the

darkened sky, and its crackle drove Azure back below the water. The last thing she needed was to get struck by lightning.

"Anyone out on the water tonight is a fool." Azure said as soon as she resurfaced. She waited for a response, knowing that they were just as foolish for braving the electricity-filled sky. Grimacing, Ocevia used her hands and tail to tread water as she continued to search for a target.

"I admit that tonight doesn't seem like it will be very fruitful. The storm is too bad. Let's hang around for a bit, though. A ship could show up."

Azure was not comfortable being out in such a turbulent storm, but she nodded anyway, and joined Ocevia in her search. She wondered if the other mermaids were out hunting, or if they were the only ones dumb enough to chance it.

Just as she pondered if they were alone, the water bubbled from beneath them. It was their only, albeit brief, warning before Oona and Lucia, the sociopathic mermaids who made up Goddess Miris' inner circle, surfaced. Their savage smirks made her blood boil.

"This is our spot," Azure spat at them. "You need to find another location." She never hesitated to mouth off to the duo, even though she knew they were dangerous.

Oona's sick smile widened as her black hair floated like an ink spill around her. "You and your weak little friend do not own any of this water. We hunt where we choose. Go ahead. Try to take souls from us. It won't end well for you."

Azure's pulse quickened, her pounding heartbeat louder in her ears than the roaring thunder overhead. She readied her retort when movement in the distance caught her eye and distracted her. A merchant ship was approaching from the direction of Vidaica. Silence descended on them as they watched it approach, rocking in the violent winds.

Grabbing Ocevia's hand, Azure pulled her toward the vessel and away from their enemies. She could hear their competition behind them, but it didn't matter. Determined to reach the target first, she headed for a rock outcropping that ran along the side of the channel. Once they reached it, Azure swam in place and began to sing. Ocevia joined in, her voice weaving perfectly into the song as they created a sensual, alluring tune. She saw Oona and Lucia across the channel but could barely make out their singing over the storm. Determined to outshine the bloodthirsty duo, Azure sang louder in the hopes of getting the ship's attention first.

"Come to me,

your long-lost love,

and hold me in your arms.

The gods above,

and the goddess below,

brought me back to you."

Enjoying Song of Death? Grab it at this link to continue the story!

https://a.co/d/dHvQ87i

FOLLOW C.A. VARIAN

Sign up for C. A. Varian's newsletter to receive current updates on her new and upcoming releases, sales, and giveaways:

You can also find all stories, books, and social media pages and follow her here:

https://linktr.ee/cavarian

https://cavarian.com/

ALSO BY C.A. VARIAN

Hazel Watson Mystery Series

Kindred Spirits: Prequel

The Sapphire Necklace

Justice for the Slain

Whispers from the Swamp

Crossroads of Death

The Spirit Collector

Crown of the Phoenix Series

Crown of the Phoenix

Crown of the Exiled

Crown of the Prophecy (Coming Soon)

Mate of the Phoenix

Supernatural Savior Series

Song of Death

Goddess of Death

An Other World Series
The Other World
The Other Key
The Other Fate (coming February 2024)

My Alien Mate Series
My Alien Protector

Saving Scarlett (coming January 2024)

Second Chance with Santa (coming December 2024)

Born of Fire (coming December 2024)

Acknowledgements

I want to thank my editor, Megan, of Willow Oak Author services, for putting up with my crazy editing schedule. (At least I keep the work coming).

I would like to thank JV Arts for this gorgeous cover.

Thank you to my Personal Assistants: Jasmine, Jessica, Jordan, and Aly. I don't know what I would do without you guys.

Thank you so much to my phenomenal Street Team, Mikela Jones, Laura Farrell, Sierra Crawford, Amber Gamble, Jule Hayes, LeeRenee Musgjerd, Pyro Ember, Tasha Melton, Samantha Gentry, Chelsea Savage, Halley Peagler, Jeanann Leary, Illisa Lea, Michele Vaughan, Jessica Spain, Debbie Webb, Autumn Gresser-Chambers, Nichole Crawley, Yvonne Aguilera, Lauren Landry, Karina Serrano, Kerrie Porter, Natali Garcia, Molly Mazure, Destiny Del Palacio, Yesenia Rosado, Kass Scholes, Cortni Jo Werkema, Kira Diduck, and a few others! You guys are so good to me!

My final thank you is to my family, friends, and most of all, my readers.

Thank you for your support!

ABOUT THE AUTHOR

Raised in a small town in the heart of Louisiana's Cajun Country, C. A. Varian spent most of her childhood fishing, crabbing, and getting sunburnt at the beach. Her love of reading began very young, and she would often compete at school to read enough books to earn prizes.

Graduating with the first of her college degrees as a mother of two in her late twenties, she became a public-school teacher. As of the release of this book, she was finally able to resign from teaching to write full time!

Writing became a passion project, and she put out her first novel in 2021, and has continued to publish new novels every few months since then, not slowing down for even a minute.

Married to a retired military officer, she spent many years moving around for his career, but they now live in central Alabama, with her youngest daughter, Arianna. Her oldest daughter, Brianna, is enjoying her happily ever after with her new husband and several pups. C. A. Varian has two Shih Tzus that she considers her children. Boy, Charlie, and girl, Luna, are their mommy's shadows. She also has three cats named Ramses, Simba, and Cookie.